Books by Elmore Leonard

The Bounty Hunters	Cat Chaser
The Law at Randado	Stick
Escape from	LaBrava
Five Shadows	Glitz
Last Stand at Saber River	Bandits
Hombre	Touch
The Big Bounce	Freaky Deaky
The Moonshine War	Killshot
Valdez Is Coming	Get Shorty
Forty Lashes Less One	Maximum Bob
Mr. Majestyk	Rum Punch
52 Pickup	Pronto
Swag	Riding the Rap
Unknown Man #89	Out of Sight
The Hunted	Cuba Libre
The Switch	The Tonto Woman and
Gunsights	Other Western Stories
Gold Coast	Be Cool
City Primeval	Pagan Babies
Split Images	Tishomingo Blues
When the Women	Mr. Paradise
Come Out to Dance	The Hot Kid

ELMORE LEONARD

The Law at Randado

HarperTorch
An Imprint of HarperCollinsPublishers

HARPERTORCH
An Imprint of HarperCollins*Publishers*
10 East 53rd Street
New York, New York 10022-5299

Copyright © 1954 by Elmore Leonard, Inc.
Excerpt from *Gunsights* copyright © 1979 by Elmore Leonard, Inc.
ISBN: 0-06-001349-4

First HarperTorch paperback printing: July 2002

HarperCollins ®, HarperTorch™, and ❦™ are trademarks of Harper-Collins Publishers Inc.

Printed in the United States of America

Visit HarperTorch on the World Wide Web at www.harpercollins.com

10   9   8   7   6

The Law at Randado

1

At times during the morning, he would think of the man named Kirby Frye. The man who had brought him here. There had been others, most of them soldiers, but he remembered by name only the one called Frye. He had known him before and it had been a strange shock to see him last night.

Most of the time, though, Dandy Jim stood at the window of the upstairs jail cell and watched the street below in the cold sunlight and tried not to think of anything.

He would see riders walking their horses, then flat-bed wagons—most often with a man and woman on the seat and children at the back end with their legs swinging over the tailgate—and now and then a man leading a pack mule. They moved both ways along the street that appeared narrower from above with the ramadas making a shadow line along the building fronts.

Saturday morning and the end of a trail drive brings all kinds to town. The wagon people, one-loop ranchers and their families who would be on their way home before dark. A few prospectors down out of the Huachucas who would drink whisky while their money lasted, then buy some to take if their credit was good. And the mounted men, most of them on horses wearing the Sun-D brand— a D within a design that resembled a crudely drawn flower though it was meant to be a sunburst—men back from a month of trail driving, back from pushing two thousand cows up the San Rafael valley to the railhead at Willcox, twenty days up and ten back and dust all the way, but strangely not showing the relief of having this now behind them. They rode silently, and men do not keep within themselves with a trail drive just over and still fresh in their minds.

Dandy Jim knew none of this, neither the day nor why the people were here. Earlier, he had watched the street intently. When he first opened his eyes, finding himself on the plank floor and not knowing where he was, he had gone to the window and looked out, blinking his eyes against the cold sunlight and against the throbbing in the back of his head that would suddenly stab through to above his eyes.

But the street and the store fronts told him only that this was no Sonoita or Tubac or Patagonia, because he had been to those places. Now he looked out of the window because there was nothing else to do, still not understanding what he saw or re- membering how he came here.

Dandy Jim was Coyotero Apache; which was the reason he did not understand what he saw. The throbbing in his head was from tulapai; and only that much was he beginning to remember.

His Coyotero name was Tloh-ka, but few Americans knew him by that. He had been Dandy Jim since enlisting as a tracker with the 5th Cavalry. They said he was given the name because he was a favorite with the men of the "Dandy 5th" and they called him Jim, then Dandy Jim to associate him with the regiment, because to say Tloh-ka you had to hold your tongue a certain way and just to call an Apache wasn't worth all that trouble. Tloh-ka was handsome, by any standards; he was young, his shoulder-length hair looked clean even when it was not, and his appearance was generally better than most Apaches. That was another reason for his name.

He slept again for a short time, lying on his stomach on the bunk, a canvas-covered wooden frame and an army blanket, but better than the floor. He opened his eyes abruptly when he heard the footsteps, but did not move his face from the canvas.

Through the bars he saw two men in the hallway. One was fat and moved slowly because of it. He carried something covered over with a cloth. The other was a boy, he saw now, carrying the same thing and he stayed behind the large man, moving hesitantly as if afraid to be up here where the cells were.

As they came to his cell the Coyotero closed his eyes again. He heard the door being opened. There was whispering, then a voice said, "Go on, he's asleep." Dandy Jim opened his eyes. The boy was setting a dishtowel-covered tray in the middle of the floor. As the boy stood up he glanced at the Coyotero. Their faces were close and the boy looked suddenly straight into the open black eyes that did not blink.

"Harold!" The boy backed away.

"What's the matter?"

"He's awake!" The boy was in the hallway now.

"We let them do that," the fat one who was called Harold said, and locked the door again.

They went to the other cell and the boy took the tray while Harold unlocked the door. The boy went in quickly and put the tray on the floor, not looking at the two Mexicans who were lying on the bunks. The door slammed and they were moving down the hall again. Dandy Jim could hear the boy whispering, then going down the stairs Harold was telling him something.

The Coyotero sat up and ate the food: meat and bread. There was coffee, too, and after this he felt better. The throbbing in his head was a dull pain now and less often would it shoot through to his eyes. The food removed the sour, day-old taste of tulapai from his mouth and this he was more thankful for than the full feeling in his stomach. And now he was beginning to remember more of what had happened.

He heard the cell door close again, this in his mind. It was dark and he was lying on the floor and now he remembered the men leaving, one of them carrying a lamp. They walked heavily and the floor against his face shook with their walking. Then darkness, and silence, and when he opened his eyes again he was here. But before that—

Tulapai. No, before that.

It came to him suddenly and his mind was not ready for it. The shock of memory stiffened his body, then left him limp the next moment and he groaned, closing his eyes tight to squeeze the picture of it from his mind. He saw her face clearly. She was on the ground and he was astride her, holding her arms with his knees. Her eyes were open wide, but she did not scream, not until he drew the knife, and holding her head down by the hair, slashed off part of her nose.

It was the fault of the tulapai, the corn beer he had been drinking as he rode home; but it was also his rage. The shock of seeing her with Susto. Across the stream, through the willow branches, seeing the two of them lying close to each other. He was halfway across the stream when they saw him. Susto ran for the brush thicket and disappeared;

but Dandy Jim's wife ran to their jacale, as if she knew she would be caught, but should at least run at a time like this. And that was where he found her and did what he had to do, what had been the customary act of a cheated Apache male longer than anyone could remember. A woman without a nose would not easily fall into adultery again.

And now he remembered more of the things that had happened the evening before: sitting with his friends drinking tulapai, drinking too much while they told him what he had done was the right thing. Then the sudden warning that soldiers were approaching the rancheria; but it was hard to think, even then with the tulapai, and they made noise fleeing on their ponies. Their minds would not calm long enough to think out their escape and do it properly. So they just ran, and all the time, for hours, the soldiers were never more than a mile behind. Just before dark the soldiers caught up and shot Dandy Jim's pony and that was the end. He remembered walking, stumbling, between their horses for a long time until they reached a place that was light and there was much noise.

And he remembered briefly, vaguely seeing a man he had once known, Kirby Frye. Then up the stairs . . . the plank floor of the cell, then daylight and the sour taste of tulapai.

He did not know what had happened to his companions. Perhaps they are still fleeing, he thought.

With the darkness they could have escaped the soldiers. And that one whose name is Frye . . . he was there. I have not seen him for a long time. But he is not here now.

He looked at the two Mexicans in the cell across the hallway. One of them was eating, but the other man was still lying on the bunk with his arm over his eyes. For a moment the Coyotero wondered why they were there.

Downstairs, the boy was talking to Harold Mendez. His name was Wordie Stedman; he was eleven and he liked better than anything else to sit in the jail office with Harold Mendez or Kirby Frye and have them tell him things. Sometimes he got upstairs; like just a while ago when Harold let him carry one of the trays. The boy had an excuse to stay there now. He had to wait for the prisoners to finish eating before he could take the trays back to the Metropolitan Café.

He said to Harold, who was middle-aged and at this moment looked comfortable in the swivel chair with his feet propped on the desk edge, staring out the window, "I'm glad I got a chance to see them close-up. They really look mean, don't they?"

Harold Mendez said, "Everybody looks that way when they wake up."

"Those two Mexicans, I saw them the other day when Kirby brought them in. One with his hat gone, shot smack off his head." Wordie grinned. "Kirby must've been off a ways else he'd a hit him."

"Maybe he was aiming at the hat."

"Why would he do that?" the boy said. "When you catch two men stealing other people's cattle you might as well aim a little lower and save the county some hangin' expenses."

"How much does it cost to hang a man, Wordie?"

"What?"

"You've been overhearing your father." Harold Mendez, the jailer, lighted a cigar now and drew on it gently, holding it the way a man does who considers cigar smoking a luxury.

"The one in the other cell'd scare the wits out of anybody," Wordie Stedman said.

"Dandy Jim?"

"That 'Pache."

"He's considered a nice-looking boy."

Wordie nodded, indicating upstairs. "There wasn't anything nice about him a while ago. He stunk to high heaven."

"I'll see he gets a bath and rinses out his mouth," Harold Mendez said.

The boy was thinking, looking absently at the stairway, then he said, "I'll bet he murdered somebody and Kirby come up and caught him red-handed!"

"The only thing he was murdering was his stomach."

The boy looked at the jailer, frowning and twisting the corner of his mouth. "He was drinking tulapai," Harold Mendez explained. "Soldiers from Huachuca out looking for stills found him and some others with tulapai. They chased after the Indians, about six braves, to get them to tell where the stills are, but Dandy Jim's the only one they caught."

"What are they doing with him here?" the boy said.

"He was close by when they caught him, so they asked Kirby if they could keep him here while they chased after the others."

The boy said excitedly, "And Kirby went along to give them a hand!"

Harold Mendez nodded. "Of course."

"He'll find them," the boy said confidently.

"What if he doesn't?"

The boy looked at the big jailer. "What do you mean?"

Harold Mendez shrugged. "I mean what if he doesn't bring them back?"

Wordie looked at him, frowning again. " 'Course he'll bring them back."

"I've known him to come home empty-handed."

"Nobody's perfect," the boy said. But if that's true, the boy was thinking, then Kirby Frye's sure the closest thing to being it. He said now, "Should I get the trays?"

"We'll give them a few more minutes."

"I don't see how they can eat. In jail." The boy went to the window and looked out just for something to do. "There's sure a lot of people here today."

"It's Saturday," Harold Mendez said.

The boy turned to Mendez suddenly. "The Sundeen crew's back."

"So I heard."

The boy seemed disappointed that what he said wasn't news, but he tried again, saying, "I'll bet there's something you don't know."

"There might be," Harold Mendez said.

"They haven't been paid off yet."

Mendez turned his head to look at the boy. "No, I didn't know that."

Wordie Stedman grinned. "I heard my dad talking about it a while ago with Mr. Tindal. Says they moved that big herd all the way up to the railhead, come all the way back, and still haven't been given their trail wages."

"Your dad say why?"

"No, but Mr. Tindal said a man does that just once and then he finds himself without a crew. Even a man like Phil Sundeen. Mr. Tindal said Old Val Sundeen used to always pay off the hands when they reached the railhead, like it should be. He said

Phil better take some lessons from his dad pretty soon if he wants to stay in the cattle business. Said if Phil minded his ways instead of drinking and carousing he wouldn't be losing stock and refusing to pay rightful trail wages."

"What did your dad say to that?"

"Mr. Tindal was doing most of the talking. My dad would just nod his head. I never seen my dad or Mr. Tindal look so worried."

"They might have good cause," Harold Mendez said. He drew on his cigar thoughtfully and his hand idly fingered a name-plate shingle that was on the desk. Harold Mendez had carved the lettering on it himself, an inscription that read: KIRBY FRYE, and under it: DEPUTY SHERIFF—RANDADO. It had taken him almost a month to carve it.

2

Across the street, in De Spain's cardroom, R. D. Tindal was about to make a speech.

He had begun forming the words in his mind the night before as he lay in his bed staring at the darkness and because of it he did not fall asleep until long after midnight. In the morning, as soon as he opened his eyes, he began recalling the words, hearing his own voice as it would sound, going over and over again the opening sentence that had to sound natural. No, more than natural, casual; but words that would hold them right from the start, words he would speak dryly in a sort of don't-give-a-damn way, an off-the-cuff understatement, but loaded with meaning. Eating his breakfast he smiled thinking of the reaction. They wouldn't laugh when he said it, because he wouldn't; but they'd shake their heads thinking: By God, that R. D. Tindal's something! His wife watched him from the stove; his daughter, Milmary, watched him while she drank her coffee, and neither of them spoke. Opening the

store, The R. D. Tindal Supply Company, and waiting on the first Saturday morning customers, he
went over the other things he would say, even an-
ticipating questions and forming the exact words
for the answers. At ten o'clock he put on his hat
and coat and told Milmary to hold down the fort
till he got back. Milmary asked him where he was
going and did it have anything to do with his being
so quiet all morning?

Going out the door he said, significantly, "Milmary, the Citizens Committee." That was all.

And now he looked at the men at his table and
the ones beyond at the other three tables and the
men over against the wall, De Spain, one of them,
standing with his back to the closed door and his
hand behind him on the knob. He stood by the
door, in case he was wanted out front. Saturday his
saloon did good business even in the morning. And
in the cardroom they could hear the sounds of the
good business, the boots and the chairs scraping
and the whisky-relaxed laughter.

R. D. Tindal wished they'd be quiet, these men
laughing over nothing, only because it was Saturday. His eyes returned to the three men at his
table—Earl Beaudry, landowner, probably his closest friend. George Stedman, manager of the Randado Branch of the Cattlemen's Bank, a good man
to know. And Haig Hanasian, owner of the Metro-

politan Café, a man you'd never know in seven hundred years, Tindal thought—and then he was ready to begin.

He cleared his throat. He had not intended to, because there was a chance someone might think he was nervous, but it just came out. He remembered though to sound casual and began by saying, "Gentlemen, it just occurred to me a minute ago, watching you boys file in, that there isn't one of us here who hasn't been shaving at least twenty years." He watched some of them finger their chins, as he had known they would. "Yet those people up to the county seat would have a special representative down here just for wiping our noses if we'd let them."

He paused to give them time to shake their heads and appreciate fully this dry, spur-of-the-moment humor.

Beaudry, Stedman and Haig Hanasian kept their eyes on Tindal, but did not shake their heads, not even faintly.

Across the room De Spain shook his head, but he was thinking: He isn't even a good actor.

Tindal leaned forward resting his elbows on the table and said, "Now I think we're all old enough to take care of ourselves, regardless of what opinion the people up to the county seat hold." He paused again, but not so long this time. "Which means we're old enough to take care of our own affairs right here in Randado without crying help from the county. Isn't that right, Earl?"

Earl Beaudry looked up. "Absolutely."

Tindal went on, "Earl's lived right here for a long time, even before there was a Randado, and his dad before that, one of the first men in the Territory. Now I'd say a man like Earl Beaudry should have a *few* words to say about how his town affairs are run. There are others of you who've been out here almost as long, got your roots planted firm now. There are some who've been here only a few years, like our friend George Stedman, but men who're damn well the backbone of the community." R.D. Tindal's mouth formed a faint grin. "What do you say, George? You think we're old enough to wipe our own noses?"

George Stedman grinned back. "I don't see why not."

De Spain blew his nose and every man in the room looked at him stuffing the handkerchief into his pocket again. He said to Tindal, "You'll have to excuse me. I've got to get back to work."

"Wait a minute now," Tindal said. "This is important."

"This is Saturday."

Tindal glanced around the room, leaning on his arms. "I'd say the question we're discussing is a shade weightier than whether or not some hands get drunk."

De Spain nodded resignedly. "All right, but get to the point."

Tindal gave him a stare, took time to suck at his teeth, then leaned back as slowly as he could. "Three days ago," he began, "our sheriff brought in single-handed two men caught in the act of rustling Sun-D stock." He grinned. "That wasn't too hard for Kirby, doing it alone. You know he's a Randado boy, done most of his growing up right here." Seriously again. "But we had something to say about signing on Kirby. Pima County give him to us as a deputy, but by God our committee passed on him! We looked over this Kirby Frye, along with others, and accepted him only after we were sure he qualified. He's young, but he's a hard-working boy and we know he can do the job. See what I mean? This committee took hold of the problem and we come up with the best deputy in the county!" Now get to the point, quick.

"Kirby Frye, Deputy Sheriff of Randado, brought in two men caught stealing cattle from a citizen of Randado . . . yet we have to wait until John Danaher's good and ready to send for the two outlaws before they're tried. We sit here waiting on the whim of a county sheriff eighty-five miles away from us." Now give 'em the big casino! "Gentlemen, here's the point. We sit here doing nothing while we're damn-right able to handle it ourselves!"

Earl Beaudry and George Stedman both nodded.

From the door De Spain said, "When was Phil Sundeen talking to you?"

Tindal looked at him, momentarily surprised, because this wasn't one of the questions he had anticipated, and feeling a sudden embarrassment he kept his eyes steadily on De Spain's dark face as if to prove that he was sincere and he said, "Do you think I'm trying to hide something? I'm not denying we talked to Phil Sundeen. I was coming to that . . . if you'd give me time to tell it my own way. Maybe I'm not a polished enough speaker for you!"

De Spain shook his head. "I'm sorry. Go ahead."

"I'm trying to do a job that could be a damn sight pleasanter. I don't see anybody volunteering to head this committee."

"You're doing a fine job," George Stedman said encouragingly. "Go ahead, tell them the rest."

"If this is an imposition on Mr. De Spain, maybe we should meet somewhere else," Tindal said.

De Spain said nothing.

George Stedman spoke up. "Go on with the rest."

R. D. Tindal cleared his throat and was embarrassed again and swore at De Spain in his mind. He said, almost angrily now, "Those two Mexicans over in the jail belong to Randado, that's what I'm getting at. And it's *our* duty to see justice done to them . . . nobody else's!" He brought his fist down on the table for emphasis.

Earl Beaudry half turned in his chair to look at the others. "You see, we—George and R.D. and me—were talking to Phil Sundeen last night. He come back last night, you know—"

Tindal interrupted, his face flushed, "Wasn't I telling it all right?"

Beaudry turned to him. "Sure, R.D. Go ahead."

"If you want to take over, Earl—"

Beaudry waved his palm toward Tindal. "You tell it, R.D."

"As Earl said, we talked to Phil Sundeen last night here in town . . . in fact we were over to the Metropolitan when they brought in that drunk Apache. That right, Haig?" This was to show that they had met Phil Sundeen in a public place and there was nothing undercover about it.

Haig Hanasian nodded. He was dark with a heavy drooping mustache and his eyes appeared half closed because the lids were heavy.

"Haig saw us," Tindal said. "So did his wife. Well, we mentioned to Phil how Kirby Frye brought in the two Mexicans; which he hadn't heard about. Then he reminded us of something we'd known for a long time. He said his stock's always been rustled. With the border so close it's a temptation and his spread's hit harder than the ones up the valley. He said he'd complained to Mendez—that's when Harold was deputy—but nothing was ever done about it. Phil said he's always had the suspicion Harold Mendez never did anything because the outlaws were always up from across the border and Harold being about ninety-nine percent Mex didn't give a particular damn so long as they were stealing from white men.

"Well, we got rid of Harold Mendez and got us a Randado boy, one we can trust. Harold Mendez isn't going to bother anybody being jailer." Tindal grinned. "With what it pays, Harold's the only one willing to do that kind of work." This was Tindal's view, not something Sundeen had told him.

"I told Phil how Kirby was deputy now. He didn't know that because he'd already started his drive the time we appointed Kirby. Then Phil made a pretty good point. He said, 'All right, let's say this new sheriff does grab a rustler. He's carted up to Tucson for trial. The man he stole from has to leave his work for at least a week, maybe longer, and go all the way up to the county seat to testify. Chances are, the rustler's only given a term in Yuma and in a year or so he's back driving stock over the border again.' That's what Phil said and by God I think it makes some sense."

Tindal leaned forward in his chair. He remembered well how he was to say this next part. He looked over the room slowly and then said, "Now what would there be to stop us—I mean *us*—from trying those two Mexicans?" The room was still silent and he added, quietly, "Right here and now."

Some of the men, looking at each other now, started to talk and one man's voice, above the others was saying, "Now wait a minute!"

Earl Beaudry turned in his chair. "Well why not?" And a man at another table shrugged and said, "That's right. When you get down to it, why not?"

George Stedman said, "Like R.D. mentioned this is a crime committed against a citizen of Randado. Now common sense would tell us that the citizens of Randado, as a body, ought to be qualified to see that justice is administered."

The man in the back who had spoken now said, "We'd be nothing more than a lynch mob."

Earl Beaudry said, "We're going to try them first."

George Stedman brought his fist down on the table. "If we're a lynch mob then that's what the court up at the county seat is, that's what any court is if you look at it that way. Can't you see we're talking as the people, and there isn't any court on the face of the earth that's more than that!"

R.D. Tindal waved his hand in the air. "Gentlemen." He said louder, "Gentlemen, here's the point. Why should we let outlaws take advantage of us, just because the courthouse is eighty-five miles away? We establish law here, deal with those two Mexicans ourselves, and then, by God, others will think twice about stealing out of the San Rafael valley!"

De Spain said, "R. D.," and when Tindal looked at him, "I don't mean to sound disrespectful, but I've got a suspicion you're asking us to do another man's work."

"We all live here!" Tindal said angrily.

De Spain shrugged. "You can make it sound like whatever you like. But . . . on the chance of sounding blunt, I'd say you were kissing Sundeen's hind end."

Tindal colored, but he kept control of himself because everyone in the room was watching him and he said, "You've always had a notion you can say whatever enters your head. Now that might be a pretty funny thing you said, but just what does it mean?"

"I'd have to draw a picture," De Spain said, "to make it plainer."

Tindal was still controlled, but with an effort. "Maybe I'm just so dumb I have to have it spelled out."

"Well," De Spain said. "Whether he looks it or not, Sundeen's the biggest man in the San Rafael. He's got the most land, he hires the most men and, what should have been said first, he's got the most money. Now being friends with a man like that can make you feel pretty important, and have some advantages besides."

Earl Beaudry grinned, shaking his head. "You been drinking your bar whisky."

"Earl," De Spain said, "I understand you lease winter graze to the Sundeens and haven't worked a day in your life. What if Phil was to lease it somewhere else?"

De Spain looked at Tindal now. He wanted to accuse him of scheming to marry his daughter off to Phil, but that might be going too far, so he just said, "To some people feeling important's the best feeling in the world." He looked at Stedman to include him.

George Stedman was composed. He said, "Since you mention dealing with Sundeen, where would you be if he and his men stopped drinking whisky?"

"I happen to have the only saloon in town."

"Well, let's say someone borrowed enough money from my bank to open another."

"I've taken the bar apart before," De Spain answered, "and thrown it in a wagon."

"Gentlemen," R. D. Tindal said. "Let's stop talking nonsense." He looked at De Spain. "We're discussing a judicial system for our citizens, nothing else, regardless of how you want to twist our words."

De Spain shrugged. "It's your affair."

"Then you don't want to be on the committee?"

"I never was, really." De Spain added, "You picked a good day with Kirby Frye away."

"Kirby'd be with us a hundred percent."

"You know damn well that's not true."

Tindal ignored him and looked at the others. "I don't think the loss of one man's going to hurt us any. If anybody else objects, speak up now. If not, nominations are open for City Judge. Next, City Prosecutor." That was the way to do it, fast. Then there wouldn't be unnecessary arguing.

Haig Hanasian stood up. He said, "I won't be a part of this." De Spain opened the door, stepping aside, and Haig went out without saying another word.

Tindal waited. Three other men left hurriedly and Tindal put their names down in his memory. When the room was quiet again he said, "All right, nominations are now open for City Judge."

Dandy Jim saw more people as noontime approached. Most of the men seemed to be entering and leaving the building directly across the street and there were many of them standing in the ramada shade, more there than anywhere up or down the street; just standing, talking to each other with their hands in their pockets and sometimes spitting out into the sun of the street. There were two buildings here, both adobe, but only the different signs indicated that there were two—DE SPAIN'S, and a little farther down, METROPOLITAN CAFÉ. Dandy Jim could not read the signs, but he put it down in his mind that these must be important places.

He thought again of the one whose name was Frye, as he had been doing from time to time. The first time he saw him had been at San Carlos when they were both much younger. He remembered the lean boy, tall and with light-colored hair with his hat off, standing watching their games. Then joining their games finally, after weeks of watching. The foot races, pony races, wrestling, and seeing how far one could run with a mouthful of water, or seeing how far a boy could travel without water at all. And even from the first, this one named Frye did well, for a white man; and he did get better.

He remembered seeing him at Fort Huachuca during the past year. Every few months this Kirby Frye would come with two Apache boys and a string of half-green horses.

Sometimes he and Frye would talk, because they remembered each other from the times they played games together and the few times in between when they would meet by chance.

Then, only a month ago, they had been together at Galluro after the raid by the renegade Chiricahuas, and Frye had gone off with the one who was called Sheriff. Dan-a-her was his name.

And now Kirby Frye was here, or at least he had

been last night. I would like to talk to him again, Dandy Jim thought. He is an easy man to talk to.

The two Mexicans, who were in the cell across from Dandy Jim, spoke to each other very little. They were here because a man in La Noria—it had been in the cantina—told them how easy it was to steal cattle from this ranch that was so large its riders could never be watching all of it. Drive the cattle across the border, the man told them, down to the Hacienda of the Mother of God. The Mayordomo there will pay good money and ask no questions. Even eat some of the beef yourselves, the man told them.

The younger of the two Mexicans spoke only a few words during the morning and only touched the fork to his food, because he was trying to picture what would happen to them. The other man, who wore a mustache and now needed a shave badly, had slept well, had eaten all of his morning meal and now looked forward to the next. He thought most often of the present, sometimes the past, if it was a pleasant remembrance, never of the future.

The younger man asked, "What will they do to us?" He was frowning and talking to himself as much as he was to his companion.

The other man said, with finality, "Shoot us." He was tired of hearing this question asked.

The younger man looked up, with fear clearly on his face. "But won't we be given a trial?"

"How would I know that?"

"You've lived in this country before."

The older man was so tired of this conversation now that he did not bother to answer. But as he looked about for something to interest him he saw, across the hallway in the other cell, Dandy Jim. He said to the younger man, "Ask that barbarian there. He's lived here all of his life."

"Here comes Sundeen!" Wordie Stedman said, turning his head from the window.

Harold Mendez drew on his cigar. He was thinking: I'm glad I'm no longer deputy. In about an hour I would have to go over to De Spain's and ask Phil to stop firing his pistol . . . and probably get the barrel across my skull. Kirby hasn't had to do that yet. But the time will come.

"There're two men with him," Wordie said.

"One of them is Digo," Harold said, though his back was to the window.

The boy nodded, looking out of the window again. "I don't know who the other one is."

"It could be anyone."

"He don't look like a trail hand."

Harold Mendez swiveled in his chair. He saw the three men dismounting in front of De Spain's and Sundeen and the one they did not know handing the reins to Digo who led the horses away, probably taking them to the livery.

"He's new," the boy said. "I never saw him before."

Harold Mendez nodded, studying the man stepping up on the porch with Sundeen. No, he wasn't a trail hand, but he wasn't a doctor or a lawyer either. Harold Mendez thought: What is there about a man like that which singles him out? I would be willing to bet my pay for a year this one is hired for his gun. Still, even thinking this, he wasn't afraid; because he knew he would never be a bother to this man.

The boy said, "Who do you think he is?"

"Just a friend of Phil Sundeen's."

"He don't look like a trail hand though, does he?"

"No, he doesn't."

"Know what he looks like to me?"

"What?"

"A gambler."

"What do they look like?"

"Always wearin' a full suit and face pale from never being in the sun."

"You couldn't tell from here whether he was pale or not."

"Well, what else might he be?"

"He could be lots of things."

"Now here comes Digo back. Boy, he's big!" Wordie said. As if looking for an argument he added, "You know he's the best horsebreaker in the whole Territory."

Harold Mendez shrugged. "He's killed as many as he's broken."

"Boy, he's fast! I've seen him in that mesquite corral. One minute talking to the bronc real sweet, close up to the bronc's ear . . . the next minute clobberin' it across the nose with one of them big fists of his. Boy—" Wordie Stedman shook his head, grinning with admiration.

After a minute, the boy said, "Can I help you get the trays now?"

"I suppose it's time." Harold Mendez came out of the chair slowly, with an effort.

Then the boy said, "Here they come back out already!" Harold Mendez looked toward the window. "And there's my dad and Mr. Tindal and Mr. Beaudry—"

Mendez saw them stepping down out of the shadow of the ramada, crossing the street, coming directly for the jail and he said to Wordie Stedman, though he wasn't sure why, "Boy, you better scat out of here!"

Wordie Stedman opened the door. "Dad—"

"Wordie! What're you doing here?" George Stedman was in the lead with Tindal and Beaudry.

"Just talking to Harold."

"Kirby Frye's not here?"

Tindal scowled. "You know he rode out last night."

"I'm making sure," Stedman said. Then to the boy, "Go on home, Wordie."

The boy frowned. "I was supposed to help Harold get the dinner trays in a minute."

Tindal said, "You let Harold do his own work . . . what he's paid for."

"Go on home now, Wordie," George Stedman said. The boy started to back away, then was walking sideways as Stedman looked over his shoulder. Behind him were Phil Sundeen, Digo and the new man whom Phil had introduced as Clay Jordan.

"He wants to be a sheriff when he grows up," Stedman said smiling. The three men behind him did not smile, but Phil Sundeen's eyes lifted and he said, "There's Mendez, the son of a bitch."

At one time Harold Mendez smiled often. He used to say, "Good morning, Mr. Stedman. Good morning, Mr. Tindal." Smiling. "Yes, sir, it certainly is a fine day." Get on the right side of the town's leading citizens and you're on your way. Now, standing in the doorway, he looked at them sullenly, his eyes on the men in front, but seeing Phil Sundeen and the new man, being conscious of the men behind them and the crowd that was gathering, and he said, "What do you want?"

"We want your two prisoners," R. D. Tindal announced.

"Which two?"

"The chilipickers," Earl Beaudry said.

"Which two are they?"

"The Mexicans."

"What for?"

Beaudry said, "To lynch 'em, for cry-sake!"

This wasn't the way to go about it and Tindal said, "By the power vested in my office as city prosecutor, I order you to hand over the two Mexican outlaws."

"City prosecutor?"

Tindal nodded his head once. "City prosecutor. George Stedman now presides over our municipal bench."

Harold Mendez frowned.

"Harold, we'll explain this just once. Not a half hour ago the Citizens Committee elected everything we need to try persons accused of crimes in Randado or against Randado citizens. George Stedman is judge. I'm prosecuting attorney. We called a jury to hear the case of those two Mexicans. Well, they heard it, Mr. Sundeen's testimony and all . . . and they rendered a prompt, just decision."

Harold Mendez shook his head. "I don't work for you. I take orders from Kirby Frye. He takes orders from Danaher, and Danaher said keep the prisoners here until he sends for them. Kirby will be back some time today. If you want to take this up with him, all right. It's none of my business."

George Stedman felt the crowd behind him and

seeing just the one man in the doorway he felt foolish. "Harold, stop wasting time and bring those
prisoners down. Representatives of this town, the
most qualified people in the world to pass sentence
on those two men, did just that. Now it's time to
administer justice."

Harold Mendez shook his head. "I want it down
on the record that I'm opposing this."

Someone in the crowd said, "It'll be down on
your tombstone."

There was scattered laughter.

Phil Sundeen pushed Tindal and the storekeeper
lurched forward almost off balance. "Step up to
him."

Digo grinned and pushed Beaudry and Stedman,
a big hand behind each man.

"Go on," Sundeen said. "Use your authority."

"Look, Harold," Tindal said. "We've explained
it to you. We didn't have to, but we did so you'd
understand what we're doing is legal. This is the
same as a court order, Harold. Now if you had a
court order given to you you'd hand those prisoners over fast."

Harold Mendez said, as if they were words he
had memorized. "I take orders from Kirby Frye,
who takes orders from John Danaher, who takes
orders from the Pima County authorities. If you
want to talk to Kirby, all right. It's none of my
business."

Phil Sundeen looked over his shoulder and said, "What time is it?"

The man called Clay Jordan, who was now standing a few steps to the side with his thumbs hooked in the gun belt beneath his open coat, moved his left hand and drew his watch from a vest pocket.

"Ten minutes shy of twelve."

"It's getting on dinnertime," Sundeen said thoughtfully. He was squinting in the morning sunlight; a bright sun, but with little warmth now at the end of November. Looking at Harold Mendez again, he said, "Digo, you think you can get Harold out of that doorway by yourself?"

Digo did not bother to answer. He pushed between Beaudry and Stedman, going for the doorway, and as he neared it Harold Mendez, who had been standing with his feet apart watching him, stepped back into the office. Digo turned his head to glance at Sundeen, then followed Harold Mendez inside. The jailer stood in front of the desk stiffly.

"Sit down," Digo said.

"It's all right."

Digo shifted his body suddenly and swung his left fist hard into the jailer's face. Mendez went back against the desk and holding himself there groped for the arm of the chair. Blood was coming from his nose as he turned the chair and eased himself into it.

Digo went to the door and called out, "He says come in."

Sundeen came first, but he stepped back inside the door to let Tindal, Stedman and Beaudry pass him. Clay Jordan was next, but he did not come in. He said, "You don't need me." Only that. Sundeen watched him walk away, going wide around the people in the street, then up into the shade in front of De Spain's, then inside.

I shouldn't have let him do that, Sundeen thought. But now he was looking at the people and he saw in the crowd, and over across the street in front of De Spain's, many of his riders. He called out, "You Sun-D men, get over here!"

In the crowd a few of them started to come forward, but stopped when someone called out, "When do we get paid?"

"You don't do what I tell you, you never will!" Sundeen answered.

They came forward out of the crowd, almost a dozen men, and stood restlessly in front of Sundeen.

"Where are the others?"

One of the men shrugged. "I don't know."

Sundeen's gaze went to the people in the street again and his eyes singled out one man standing near the front, a lean man with his hatbrim low over his eyes and a matchstick in the corner of his mouth. Merl White, one of his riders.

"Merl, what's the matter with you?"

"Nothin'."

"Get over here."

"I don't work for you no more," Merl White said. He stood his ground and did not move.

"Since when?"

"Since you stopped paying wages."

Sundeen smiled. "You don't have enough patience."

"I lost it," Merl said. "I can name three or four more lost theirs."

"Who are they, Merl?"

"You'll find out."

Sundeen's mouth still bore part of the smile. "Tell you what, Merl. You and those other three or four meet me over to De Spain's when I'm through here and I'll pay you off."

Merl kept his eyes on Sundeen and he said, "We'll be there."

Tindal was next to Sundeen in the doorway. He called out, "Where're the rest of you committeemen?" A few men came toward him, then behind them more were pushing through the crowd. "Get in here!"

"That's the ticket," Sundeen said. He slapped Tindal on the shoulder and moved back into the office. "What happened to him?" He nodded toward Harold Mendez.

"He got a nosebleed," Digo answered.

"Where're the keys?"

"Right here." Digo held them up.

Sundeen looked at Tindal. "You think you can do the rest?"

Tindal hesitated, but he said, "Of course we can."

"Like hell." Sundeen shoved past him and started up the stairs, Digo behind him and the rest of them following.

The Sun-D riders and the committeemen who had come inside moved up the stairs now, hurrying in the noise of dozens of boots on the narrow stairway and suddenly there was an excitement that could be felt; it came with the noise and the hurrying and there was an anxiousness inside of each man now, the last ones not wanting to be last, going up the stairs two at a time to be a part of the excitement, not wanting to miss anything now that it was underway and everybody was in on it. Suddenly a man felt himself very much a man and the ones who had reached the upper floor first stood with their hands on their hips waiting for all the stragglers to come up, looking at the two Mexicans who were both standing, but well back from the bars, and then looking at the Apache in the other cell who stood by the window, but with his back to it.

A man who had never seen either of the Mexicans before spat on the floor and yelled, "Pull them bean-eaters the hell out!"

They crowded in front of the cell, looking

through the bars at the two Mexicans who stood close together staring at the crowd with their mouths foolishly, wonderingly open; then the younger one wetting his lips, his eyes going over the crowd of men, wetting his lips again and now his hands were clenching and unclenching with nothing to hold on to. He could feel the hot tingling in his body and his heart beating against his chest, his legs quivering—he was aware of his toes moving against the straps of his sandals—but there was nowhere to run.

The older Mexican stood dumbfoundedly, not moving his body, and as his body began to tense he tried very hard to remain calm, talking to himself very slowly, telling himself not to become excited and act like a child, but this took a great effort and it was almost unbearable.

He heard his companion's voice—"Mother of God . . . Virgin Mother of God . . ."—and for some reason he did not want these men to hear this and he rasped at the younger man, "Shut up! Hold on to yourself!" A man was opening the door now, a big man who looked Mexican but who wore the hat of a gringo—like the one who had brought the food with the boy, but it was not that one.

"Pull it open, Digo!"

The sound of metal striking metal, clear, even with the voices, then Digo saying, "This goddamn key's no good."

Someone said, "That one was praying . . . you hear him?"

"He better."

"That's the way they are . . . pull their own sisters in the stable on Saturday night, then go to church on Sunday!"

"Give me it," Sundeen said. He took the key from Digo, turned it in the lock effortlessly and pushed the door open hard making it swing clanging against the bars. "Get 'em out!"

Digo went in, pushed in with men close behind him. He jabbed his elbows making room, then took hold of the younger Mexican who had backed away, but was now against the bunk and could go no farther, grabbing the Mexican's arm and bending it behind his back.

The younger Mexican screamed out, raising himself on his toes.

"Let him walk like a man!" the other Mexican said.

Digo pushed the man he held toward the cell door and as he did came around with his clenched fist swinging wide. The mustached Mexican started to duck, but not quickly enough and the blow caught him squarely on the side of the head sprawling him over the bunk and against the adobe wall. He sat up shaking his head as Earl Beaudry and another man each took an arm and dragged him out.

Digo was grinning. "He walks strange for a man."

"Come on," Sundeen said. "Get the other one."

As Digo took hold of him again the younger Mexican said, "We are to be tried now?"

"You've been tried."

"But when?"

"What do you care when?"

Close to Sundeen, Tindal said, "Tried and found guilty by legal court action. Now, by God, take your medicine like a man!"

"But it was only a few of those cows—"

"Listen, you took a chance and lost. Now face up to it!"

"They were returned . . . every one we took!"

" 'Cause you got caught."

"Come on!" Sundeen said suddenly, with anger. "Get him out of here." He stepped aside as Digo twisted the man's arm and pushed him, raising him to his toes, through the cell door, then down the crowded hallway, pushing the Mexican hard against the men who couldn't get out of the way quickly enough.

"Don't touch me with that greaser!"

"Then get out of the way!"

Sundeen said to Tindal, "Digo's a wheel of justice."

Tindal, looking at Sundeen's beard-stubbled,

sun-darkened expressionless face, hesitated, not knowing whether to laugh or not, then just nodded.

Someone said, "What about this one?"

"That's an Indin."

"I got eyes."

"What'd he do?" a third man said.

"That's the one the soldiers brought in."

Another man said, "Fool around with army property and you get a bayonet in the ass."

"We'd be doing them a favor."

"Look at the eyes on the son of a bitch."

"Imagine meetin' him alone out on the flats. Just you and him, no horses, not another livin' soul around—"

"For cry-sake come on . . . they're taking them down already!"

Dandy Jim had not moved from the window. Without expression he watched them take the Mexicans. He heard the men talking about him, understanding only a few of their words, and a moment later the hallway was deserted, the last sounds going down the stairs.

Then suddenly voices again, a cheering from the people in the street as the men, dragging the two Mexicans, seemed to burst from the front door of the jail into the sunlight.

And now the excitement, the not wanting to miss anything, the not wanting to be left out, was in the street. It was there suddenly with the noise and the stark violence of what was taking place. People joining the crowd, running neck-straining behind the ones closer to the Mexicans, some running ahead to the livery knowing or sensing that it would take place there; and others, standing in the long line of ramada shade and in windows; a man with his family standing up in the flat bed of a wagon and their heads turning as the crowd pushed by them; those in doorways watching fascinated, wanting to see it and not wanting to see it. Some went inside. A woman shooing three children into the doorway and the little boy yelling something as she herded them.

De Spain was alone behind the bar. He had one customer, a man who drank beer slowly, sipping it, smoking and sipping beer, leaning on the bar. It was the man who had come in with Sundeen earlier. Clay Jordan. He paid no attention to what was going on outside; he did not even glance toward the windows at the noise. But when the noise was farther down the street he finished the beer and went out.

Haig Hanasian, watching from the door of his café, saw them come out of the jail. He turned away and went back to the kitchen where there was no cook now. No cook, no waitresses. And looking toward the front again, down the whitewashed adobe length of his café and through the open

doorway he could see his wife, Edith. She was
standing with one arm about a support post raising
herself on tiptoes, straining to see over the crowd;
and as he watched her, she moved out of view.

Now they were passing a sign that read R.D.
TINDAL SUPPLY Co. Milmary Tindal was standing
beneath the sign.

"Dad!"

"You go inside, Milmary."

"Dad—"

"I said go inside!"

Now they were beyond, almost to the livery stable that was set back from the corner with the
fenced yard in front and in the middle of the fence,
the main entrance gate—two upright timbers and a
cross timber over the open gate.

"We don't have ropes," Sundeen said. "Digo, get
ropes!"

"Mine?" Digo said. "That's bad luck."

"I don't care whose."

"We'll have them."

Earl Beaudry looked up at the cross timber, then
back to Sundeen. "Here, Phil?"

"Why not?'

R.D. Tindal waved his arms. "All right, you men
back! Move back and give us some elbow room."

Now the two Mexicans were lifted to their feet
to stand under the cross timber. The younger one
put his head back to look at the beam, then looked

at the crowd again, at all of the faces close in front
of him, and he began to cry. His companion told
him, for the sake of God, to shut up and to hold on
to himself.

"This is as good a place as any," Tindal said.

"How are you going to do it?" Sundeen said.

"What?"

"How do you go about hanging a man?"

"All you need is rope."

"Just tie it around their necks and yank 'em up in
the air?"

"I don't know . . . I guess I never thought about
it."

Digo came across the livery yard with a coiled
rawhide riata in each hand. He handed one to Earl
Beaudry and they began to uncoil the lines and
bend a loop into one end of each.

The older Mexican said, "Your justice is not
slow."

Close by, George Stedman said, "Nobody's talking to you."

"Listen," the older Mexican said. "You have us
now . . . and you are going to kill us. But grant one
last request."

"Go to hell."

"It isn't much. Just get a priest."

"There's no priest here."

"At La Noria," the Mexican said. "What difference does it make if you put this off a few hours?"

"If you think somebody's going to ride all the way down to La Noria to get a priest, you're crazy."

Earl Beaudry looked up. "On Saturday."

"Look," the older Mexican said. "We are going to die. Is that much to ask?"

"You should've thought of that before."

Beaudry added, "Before you stole that beef." He had tied the knot and now pulled on it, testing it.

"Whether we should have or not is past. But it remains we need a priest."

"That's tough luck," Stedman said.

The older Mexican said no more, but after a moment he leaned closer to his companion and said, "Pray. But pray to yourself."

"Who's going up?" Sundeen said, looking at the beam.

Digo grinned. "I'd break it."

"Need somebody light." Sundeen's eyes went to Tindal.

Tindal forced a smile. "My climbing days are over."

Beaudry said, "Hell, give me a boost."

Digo stooped and they helped Beaudry up onto his shoulders, steadying him, holding his legs as Digo rose slowly. He threw the lines over the beam, looping them three times, then gave each a half hitch so that with weight on the hanging end the line would be pulling against itself; and when he

came down the loops were hanging just longer than
head high to a mounted man.

Now Digo went into the livery stable. He was
gone for a few minutes and when he reappeared he
was mounted and leading two horses with bridles,
but without saddles.

"Mount 'em up," Sundeen said.

"Wait a minute."

Sundeen turned at the words behind him. Clay
Jordan was coming toward him through the crowd.
"You going to help out now?" Sundeen said.

"Nobody rides that horse." Jordan nodded to
one of the mounts Digo had brought.

"It won't be but for a minute," Sundeen grinned.

"Nobody rides him."

"You superstitious?"

"Either you tell Digo to take him back, or I do."

Sundeen shrugged. "You tell him."

Digo looked at them, not understanding.
"What's the difference?" But he saw the way Jordan was watching him and he said, "All right," and
led Jordan's horse back to the stable. When he returned with another, Jordan was no longer in the
circle beneath the cross beam.

"Let's get this over with," Stedman said.

Tindal said, "We got to tie their hands."

"What for?" Beaudry asked.

"You always do."

"It's better if you don't . . . they fight longer trying to hold their weight off the rope, then their arms give out."

Tindal frowned. "What's the matter with you?"

"This isn't a church meeting, R. D."

"You talk like a crazy man." Tindal turned from Beaudry and saw that Stedman was already tying their hands. He had cut enough length from the free ends of the riatas hanging from the beam.

Now the older Mexican said, "What about a cigarette first?"

Tying the man's hands behind his back, Stedman said, "Go to hell."

"Don't you have any customary last things?"

Digo rolled a brown paper cigarette, lit it, then placed it between the man's lips. "Here. Don't say I never gave you anything."

The Mexican inhaled and with the cigarette in the corner of his mouth blew out smoke in a slow stream. "You've given me enough already."

Digo said in Spanish, "You feel you are much man, don't you?"

"Not for long," the man answered, also in Spanish.

"It's too bad this has to happen to you."

The Mexican shrugged.

"Does your companion wish a cigarette?"

"Ask him."

Digo smiled. "He looks already in another world."

Barely above a whisper the younger one was reciting, ". . . *Santificado sea el tu nombre, venga a nos el tu reino* . . ."

Digo grinned at him and said, "Remember to have perfect contrition."

The older Mexican said suddenly, "Do this quickly and stop talking!"

Now Digo shrugged. "As you say."

They lifted the Mexicans to the bare backs of the horses and now no one in the crowd spoke. In the silence, Digo mounted. He kneed his horse in a tight circle between the two Mexicans, reached up and adjusted the loop over the older Mexican's head and tightened the honda at the nape of his neck. The younger one tried to move his head away, but Digo's hand clamped over his jaw and held the head still until he dropped the noose over it and tightened the knot.

Now he moved out behind them and dismounted. Still there was silence and he took his time, with everyone watching him, walking up close behind the two horses. In front, an opening had been cleared to let the horses run.

Digo waited for a signal, but none came. So it was up to him. All right. He raised both hands in the air, said, "Go in peace—" and brought his hands down slapping the rumps of the horses.

They swung out, then back toward him on the ropes and turning, jumping aside, Digo could hear the horses breaking away down the street. The bodies jerked on the tight lines, but only for part of a minute. He heard Tindal say, "My God, look at their pants—"

Someone else said, "I don't feel very good."

And it was over—

3

Kirby Frye rode in shortly before nine o'clock.

He tied his dun gelding in front of the jail and started for the front steps, but at the walk he thought: A few more minutes won't matter to Harold. He turned and crossed the street, walking slowly with the stiffness of all day in the saddle. He was hungry, he felt the taste for a glass of beer and he was anxious to see Milmary Tindal; all three were before him and he didn't know which to do first.

It felt good to walk and he was thinking how good the beer would taste. Sit down and stretch your legs, even before washing up, take the first glass and drink it better than half right down, though it burns your throat. Then sip what's left. Smoke a cigarette and drink the beer slow. Then have another one and sip that.

De Spain's windows, above the painted lower half, showed every lamp up to full brightness. Frye opened the door. But he closed it again and went on. Smoke and noise and he didn't feel that much like having to make conversation in a Saturday night crowd. The Metropolitan was still open, and a few doors down he saw light coming from Tindal's store. Well, he could always see Mil at home if she closed the store; but if the café closed—

He opened the door of the Metropolitan and almost bumped into the cook who was coming out.

"Too late, Ed?"

"Hello, Kirby. Too late for me."

"Can I get something?"

"Sure, Edith's still there."

"I'm starvin'."

"You get them drunk Indins?"

"All of a sudden they disappeared."

"Ain't that the way. Well . . . Edith'll fix you something. I got catchin' up to do."

"Thanks, Ed."

The café was empty. The counter was clean and most of the tables had been cleared, all but two that were near the front and still cluttered with supper dishes. With the emptiness was silence. Frye walked back toward the kitchen, hearing his steps and the metallic ching of his spurs which seemed louder because they were the only sounds in the room.

Nearing the open doorway to the kitchen a voice said softly, "Phil?"

Frye hesitated, then went into the kitchen, looking to the left. Edith Hanasian, Haig's wife, was sitting at the table against the wall with a cup of coffee in front of her.

"It's me."

"Oh." She looked at Frye with surprise.

"I wondered if I could get a bite."

"Of what, Kirby?"

"Whatever might be on the stove."

"You look tired."

"Been working all day."

"Would you like a drink?"

"That'd be fine."

"Sit down then."

Frye moved to the table. "Where's Mr. Hanasian?"

The woman shrugged. "I don't know."

"You want me to sit out front or here?"

Edith smiled. "If he didn't trust the deputy, who would he trust?"

"I just didn't know where you wanted me to sit."

"Here. Then I won't have so many steps."

Frye pulled out the chair opposite to Edith and sat down. "The coffee smells good."

"Would you rather have that?"

"I just said it smelled good."

The woman rose. She went to a cupboard and returned with an almost-full whisky bottle, picking up a glass from the serving table as she did. She placed the glass in front of him and poured whisky into it.

"Whoa—"

"You're a big boy now."

"I'm not that big." He drank some of the whisky and putting the glass down felt Edith move around next to him. She took his hat off and sailed it over to the serving table.

"I've had that on so long I forgot it was there."

"You look younger without it."

"Do I?"

She moved her fingers over his sand-colored hair. "Sometimes you look like a little boy," she said quietly.

"Do I look like a hungry one?"

She moved away, as if reluctantly. "What do you want?"

"I don't care."

"Enchiladas are still warm."

"Fine."

She went over to the stove, then looked back at him. "Or lamb stew?"

"All right. Stew."

"You're easy to please."

She placed a heaping plate of the stew in front of him, brought salt and bread, then sat down again.

"Tastes good."

"Does it?" She was leaning forward now with her elbows on the table, watching him eat. He glanced at her and the way she was leaning he could see the beginning of the hollow between her breasts. She was an attractive woman, not more than a year past thirty, but she smiled little. It showed in the way her mouth was set and in the eyes that seemed indifferent to whatever they looked at. Probably in another few years she would be fat. Now, there was only the hint of it, a pleasing softness that would become too soft.

"Where'd you say your husband was?"

"I said I didn't know."

"That's right." He ate the stew, pushing it onto the fork with a piece of bread, dabbing the bread in the gravy and eating that. When he was finished he wiped the plate clean this way.

"More?" Edith asked.

Frye looked at her still leaning close to the table. Then he began rolling a cigarette. "I wouldn't mind a cup of coffee . . . though I hate to ask you to move."

Edith smiled, still not moving. "Sometimes the little boy in you begins to disappear."

"Do you want me to get it?"

She rose then. "You're paying for it."

He watched her go to the stove and come back with the coffeepot.

"I thought eating in the kitchen like this I was a guest."

She poured them each a cup and sat down, but now she sat sideways in the chair, leaning against the wall, looking from the ceiling to the stove and at nothing in particular, not bothering to answer him.

"Business slow?"

Edith shrugged indifferently. "It's all right."

"You generally do better than this on Saturday, don't you?"

"Everybody's next door, celebrating."

"Celebrating what?"

"Their manhood."

"What?"

Edith looked at him. "Didn't you hear what happened?"

"I just got back."

"Go next door; you'll find out."

Frye shrugged. He wasn't going to beg her. He finished his coffee, stubbed out the cigarette on the plate and stood up. He was tall, but with a big-boned leanness, and he looked younger than twenty-four. "Maybe I will," he said. Then, "If I see Phil, you want me to tell him you're here?"

Edith hesitated, studying Frye's face. "Why would I want that?"

"You thought I was him when I came in."

"Don't jump to any conclusions."

"Wouldn't think of it. How much do I owe?"

"Thirty cents."

He felt inside his pants pockets. "I'll pay you to-morrow, all right?" He grinned. "I guess I didn't bring any money."

Edith shook her head. "Then the little boy comes back again."

Frye was smiling. "That's no way to talk to the deputy sheriff."

He went out the front door and stopped on the plank sidewalk to make another cigarette. The noise inside De Spain's would go on until late, dying out slowly, then the street would be quiet again. It had been quiet last night when he left. Friday night was usually quiet. He lighted the cigarette, looking across the street to the jail. Quiet as a church. He heard laughter from De Spain's.

Edith said they were celebrating—

She thought I was Phil Sundeen when I came in. That's it. Sundeen's back from his drive and his men are celebrating. Probably been at it since early this morning. Sitting in there all day drinking.

He shook his head faintly remembering this morning, miles away chasing like hell after nothing. His eyes went to the jail again. Harold would be asleep now, sitting up with his feet on the desk.

But Edith said something happened. Not just that they were celebrating, but that something happened—

Let it wait.

He flicked the cigarette into the street and moved away from the cafe.

Milmary Tindal was locking the front door of

the store when he came up behind her. She heard
the footsteps, then heard the footsteps stop and she
turned coming around hesitantly, keeping her face
composed, then her features relaxed suddenly and
she smiled with relief.

"Kirby! You scared—"

Holding her shoulders he kissed her unexpectedly, his lips making a smacking sound against
hers.

"Kirby!"

"Too loud?"

"Right out on the street—"

"You look good, Mil."

She brushed a wisp of hair back from her forehead. "I'm a mess."

"You going home?"

The girl nodded, looking up at him. "When did
you get back?"

"Just a few minutes ago."

"Did you catch them?"

"This afternoon they made it over the border."

"Daddy was sure you'd get them." They started
walking along the adobe fronts, hearing behind
them faint sounds from De Spain's. Ahead were the
shadowy forms of men sitting in front of the buildings, now and then a cigarette glow in the darkness,
and passing them—"Good evening—"

"You get 'em, Kirby?"

"No, sir. They got away."

"That's too bad."

Nearer the end of the street the adobe fronts were deserted and now there was only the sound of their steps hollow on the plank sidewalk, and out behind the adobes and in the yard of the livery stable they could hear crickets.

"It's a nice night," he said.

The girl was walking with her head down watching her steps and did not answer. Standing straight she would come just past Frye's shoulder. Now she seemed smaller. Her figure was slight, almost boyish, but her face was delicately feminine: dark, almost black hair combed back from her face and small features softly pale in the darkness. They turned the corner and started up the low sweeping hill, seeing the lights farther up. They flickered in an uneven row through the trees indicating at least five or six houses.

"What's the matter?"

"Nothing," the girl said.

"You're not talking."

"Well, I'm tired. That's all."

"How's your father?"

She looked up at him suddenly. "He's fine."

"What're you so jumpy about?"

"Well, why're you asking me so many questions?"

"All day long I've been talking to a horse."

"I'm sorry."

"Has he said any more about you marrying Sundeen?"

"Of course not. I thought that was settled."

He said quietly, "I hope so."

Their footsteps were muffled and Frye's spurs chinged softly. Abruptly Milmary said, "I suppose you heard all about what happened today." In the darkness her voice seemed natural.

"You sound like Edith."

"You were with her?"

"All we talked about was supper."

"She didn't tell you?"

"Uh-uh."

"Well, there was a trial today."

"A trial?"

"Our town's first legal court action."

He was frowning. "The county judge was down here?"

Almost defensively she said, "We have our own judge and prosecuting attorney," and went on quickly now as if to tell it and get it over with. "The Citizens Committee met this morning and elected a city judge and a city prosecuting attorney."

"They don't have the—"

"Let me finish. Mr. Stedman was elected judge and my father, prosecutor. It was done legally, by vote of the Citizens Committee, and they represent all of the people here."

"You sound like your father."

"Will you please have the courtesy to let me finish?"

"Go on."

Her face was flushed now looking at Frye, who for a moment had smiled, but was now frowning again. "After the elections they decided to hold the first court session and they tried the two cattle thieves you've been holding. Phil Sundeen was made to testify even though everybody knew those two men were the ones. You said yourself you caught them driving off the cattle. So they were found guilty."

"Then what?"

Milmary hesitated. "Then they were taken out and legally hanged."

Frye was silent.

"The men felt, why should they wait for a court way up at Tucson to get good and ready before something's done. Our citizens are just as qualified . . . more so even, since it was one of our people whose stock was stolen."

"Your father explained all this?"

"Of course he explained it to me, I'm not a lawyer."

"Neither is he."

"He's got common sense!"

"Mil, you can't just set up a court any place you want. We're part of the county, protected by the county. Maybe we should have a judge and a prosecutor here, but to get them would take some doing up at Tucson, not just a self-made committee deciding in one morning."

"Kirby, those two men were guilty. You caught them yourself," she said pleadingly.

"But you can't set up the law *after* the wrong's done. You got to have the authority before. I even know that much."

"I suppose my father and Mr. Stedman aren't as intelligent as those people up at Tucson?"

"Now you're talking like a woman."

"What do you want me to talk like?"

Frye said quietly, "The point is, the law is already established to handle things like this. Everybody's agreed to it, so you can't just come along and set up your own law."

"Even if it's something we should have had a long time ago?"

She's using her father's words, Frye thought. And she wants to believe them. He said, "Where did they hang them?"

Milmary hesitated. "At the livery."

"Did you see it?"

"Part of it."

"A big crowd?"

"Of course."

"Was Harold Mendez there?"

"I didn't see him."

Frye said, "They were taken from the jail,

marched down to the livery and hanged. Just like that?"

"I didn't see all of it."

"Did the part you see look fair?"

"I don't suppose a hanging would ever look *fair*. You're using the wrong word."

"What's a better word?"

"Kirby, use some sense! They were tried by competent men and found guilty. Now it's over."

They started to walk again, slowly, and did not speak for a few minutes. Nearing the house, Frye said, "Is your father home?"

"He said he wouldn't be home till late. Kirby, what can you do about it now?"

"I don't know."

"It's over now."

"Part of it is."

Milmary said, wearily, "If you don't understand, there's no use talking about it."

"Maybe your dad can explain it to me."

Milmary did not answer. She went up the porch steps and into the house.

Harold Mendez could feel that his nose was still swollen. Now he was touching it gently, as he had been doing all afternoon and evening, still not sure whether or not it was broken, when Frye opened the door.

"I saw you tie up a while ago," Harold said,

"but by the time I got to the door you were across the street."

"I was hungry."

"Did you get them?"

"No."

"Well—"

"Everybody's more concerned with whether we got those tulapai drinkers than with what happened right here."

"You heard then."

"Milmary told me. Where're the bodies?"

"We took them down. There were two men here from La Noria who helped me. No one else I asked would."

"Did you try to stop them?"

Harold shook his head slowly. "I couldn't see any point to it. Even if I'd tried, they still would have hung them." His fingers touched his nose.

"It looks like you told somebody no," Frye said.

"Digo was showing his authority. Do you think it's broken?"

Frye looked at Harold's nose closely, feeling the bridge of it with his finger. "I don't think so."

"They came in like a flood once it started. At first only a few were doing anything. Tindal, Beaudry, Stedman . . . and Sundeen. But once it started you would have thought everybody in town was in here."

"The place looks all right."

"They didn't break anything. I don't know why, but they didn't break anything."

Frye said suddenly, "What about Dandy Jim?"

"He's still upstairs. How long are you going to hold him?"

"I don't know. It was out of their way to come back here, so they went straight to Huachuca. They'll send for him when they get ready." He was referring to the Fort Huachuca Cavalry Patrol.

"Like Danaher sending for the two cattle thieves."

Frye moved to the window thoughtfully. "Do you know if Tindal's across the street?"

"I think so. What are you going to do?"

"Talk to him, or one of the others."

"Wait a while."

"I've got to sooner or later."

"Not tonight." Harold Mendez shook his head as he spoke. "They've been over there drinking and playing poker. They even had their dinner brought in so they wouldn't have to leave."

"They're really celebrating—"

"Listen, why don't you go to bed? Then tomorrow you can talk to them one at a time."

But you don't come home, find out something like this has happened and just go to bed, Frye was thinking. They must have been drunk to do it. No . . . Sundeen. This was probably Sundeen's idea and those men would go out on a long limb to look good in his eyes. "Harold, who was the leader?"

"They say Tindal at the meeting. But he'd make speeches in an outhouse if someone would go in with him to listen."

"Sundeen then."

Harold nodded. "Tindal might think he organized it, Stedman might think his weight influenced the others . . . but it was Sundeen behind it. Sundeen drinks too much and he talks loud, but I think he watches, and he understands these men."

"When did he get back?"

"Yesterday. He came to town last night just before you left. He was in the Metropolitan with the committee heads for a long time." Harold studied Frye for a moment standing by the window. "Listen, I don't mean to sound disrespectful, this Tindal might be your father-in-law someday . . . but you know how he talks: 'Sure, General So-and-so, I remember a humorous account he told at dinner one time . . . ' Or the way he looks off in the distance sucking his teeth like he's calculating a weighty problem, and all the time he doesn't know a goddamn thing. I don't like to say that, but that's the way he is. You haven't been here long as a grownup, but you should know it yourself by now."

"You can't pick your father-in-law," Frye said.

"Like he's trying to pick his son-in-law," Harold said. "He'd give his right one to have her marry Sundeen."

"Well, that's something else. Was De Spain there?"

"I don't think so."

"Or Hanasian?"

"I don't think he was either."

"And they've been in there ever since—"

"They came out just the once."

"When?" Frye looked at him.

"I thought you'd heard."

"No."

"Did you hear about Merl White being there earlier?"

Frye shook his head.

"Merl and some others wouldn't join Phil. Merl said they'd quit because Phil hadn't paid their trail wages."

"Why not?"

"Why does Phil need a reason? Like riding his horse into De Spain's. He does what he feels like doing. Right out in front of everybody Phil told Merl to come over to De Spain's after and he'd settle up. Well, Merl went over. He and two others walked into De Spain's and a few minutes later they were carried out. The story is, Sundeen threw whisky in Merl's face, then Digo hit him. The other two stood there until Digo started at them. They each took one swing before they were on the floor. Then Digo pulled their boots off and carried them one at a time to the porch and threw them out in the street. I saw what happened after that. Sundeen came out and this new man with him—"

"Who's that?"

"Jordan. Clay Jordan."

Kirby shook his head, not knowing the name.

"They stood on the porch until Digo came with horses, then Sundeen and Digo made them run, shooting at their feet. Sundeen went back inside, but Digo and some other Sun-D riders went out after them and made them keep running until they were out of sight . . . without any shoes on."

"No one sided with Merl then?"

"Of course not."

"And nobody's gone out to find them?"

"About two hours after it happened I took a wagon and started out. I wasn't even beyond the last house when Digo rode next to me and said 'Where are you going?' "

Frye's eyes were on Harold, but he said nothing.

"I told him nowhere and turned the wagon around." Harold sat down and his fingers touched his nose, stroking it gently.

Frye was leaning against the window frame, watching him. After a moment he said, "It's all right, Harold."

"I'm not apologizing," the jailer said.

"You don't have to."

"What if I had tried to stop them? I mean before. I would be dead now. I couldn't see where it would be worth it."

"It's all right."

"You're goddamn right it is," Harold said.

"Why don't you go home now?" Frye said.

Harold looked up at him. "I'll go over with you if you want me to."

"No, you go on home."

"What are you going to do?"

"Just talk."

"Don't try to arrest them They'll laugh at you."

Frye was silent. Then he straightened and walked away from the window. "It's a hell of a thing, isn't it?"

Harold nodded. He watched Frye open the door, then he rose slowly and followed him.

4

Clay Jordan saw them first, because he was facing the open doorway. Sundeen was on Jordan's left, then around the table, Stedman, Tindal and Beaudry; Sundeen dealing cards over the stacks of poker chips in front of him, the other three watching. They were in De Spain's cardroom.

Past Tindal's right shoulder, through the doorway, down the length of floor in front of the bar to the double doors, Jordan was looking straight ahead and he saw one of the doors push in. He recognized Harold Mendez, and from that knew who the younger one, the one who came first, must be. He said nothing to Sundeen, but watched them come down the length of bar, passing Digo standing midway at the bar, Digo realizing they were there and turning to look after them. As Frye neared the doorway, Jordan's gaze went unhurriedly from the stiff-brimmed hat and the shadowed eyes to the Colt on the right hip and the hands hanging loose, then back to the eyes as Frye stopped inside the doorway.

"Mr. Tindal—"

Tindal looked over his shoulder, then smiled turning in the chair. "Kirby! Come on in, boy!"

Frye moved closer to the table. "Mr. Stedman . . . Mr. Beaudry—" He only nodded to Phil Sundeen because it had been a long time since he had seen Phil and he wasn't sure what to call him. He glanced at Jordan, then looked at Tindal again.

"Could I speak to you a minute?"

Tindal frowned. "What about?"

"This afternoon—"

"Oooh, that." Tindal's narrow face grinned. "You heard about it, uh?"

"Yes, sir."

"Well . . . I'll explain it to you tomorrow, Kirby. We're right in the middle of a hand. Sit down there and order what you want. Put it on my bill."

"I thought this might be important enough to talk about now," Frye said. He heard Stedman say, "I call," and saw him push two chips toward the pot.

"Sure it's important," Tindal said, "but it'll keep till tomorrow."

Stedman said, "What do you do, R. D.?"

Tindal glanced at his cards. "How much to stay?"

"Two dollars."

"I'm in." Tindal had less than ten chips in front

of him. He took two off the top of the stack and dropped them on the pile of chips in the middle of the table.

"Mr. Tindal, I want to find out your side—"

Beaudry threw his cards down. "I fold."

Frye glanced at Beaudry, then to Tindal again whose back was toward him now. He moved to the side so he could see Tindal's face. "I'd like to know how you could do a thing like that."

Clay Jordan pushed two chips away from him. "Some people don't know enough to go home," he said mildly. He glanced at Sundeen. "You're called."

Tindal turned his head, but did not look up at Frye. "Kirby, I said tomorrow!"

"Mr. Tindal, I can't find out something like this has happened and just go to bed and forget about it."

Jordan looked at Frye momentarily. "Maybe you better try."

Sundeen's hand slammed down on the table spilling the chips in front of him. "Goddamn it, we're playing poker!"

"All right, Phil," Stedman said quickly. He glanced at Frye. "Just a minute, Kirby." Then to Sundeen, again, "What've you got, Phil?"

Sundeen showed his hand. "A pair of ladies over," he said sourly.

"That beats me," Stedman said. He threw in his

hand watching the others and saw that they were beaten too. "All right," he said then, "let's just take a minute and explain to Kirby what we did. Now I think being deputy sheriff he's entitled to some explanation." No one spoke.

Stedman took his time now. He said, "Kirby, briefly . . . the committee met this morning. We used our own God-given authority to set up a judicial system for our city. R.D. was elected public prosecutor and I, I was honored to accept as municipal judge. Then, under the power vested in us, we tried the two outlaws you brought in. Twelve men found them guilty, Kirby. Twelve men, after R.D. presented the evidence against them. I then felt it my duty to prescribe the death sentence. For the main reason, to let it be known how we deal with outlawry and that way discourage any future crimes against Randado. Kirby, this was done with clear conscience and, as I said before, through a God-given authority."

"Mr. Stedman," Frye said, "you know better than that."

Stedman looked at him surprised, then his eyes half closed to a squint. "We're not going to argue with you, Kirby."

Suddenly it was clear and he should have known it before, but this brought it out into the open without any words wasted. They considered him of little importance. Of *no* importance! Standing by the table he had felt self-conscious with no one paying any attention to him, but now he was suddenly angry realizing why. These were older men who didn't have to listen to a boy who'd only been deputy a month and before that never in his life had an ounce worth of authority. He felt his face flush and he said, "I'm not going to argue either. Tucson gets the report first thing in the morning. You can argue with them." He turned to leave.

"Kirby!" Tindal was around in his chair. He waited, sucking his teeth, making sure Frye would stay. He saw Harold Mendez just inside the room and Digo lounging in the doorway. "Kirby . . . you're a good boy. You work hard and you keep yourself presentable . . . but"—Tindal looked him up and down carefully—"maybe you're not as smart as I thought you were."

Frye waited, with his respect for this man fading to nothing.

"We've been on this earth a little longer than you have," Tindal said, and nodded, indicating the men at the table. "And I think maybe we've collected a little more common sense and judgment. That's nothing *against* you, Kirby, it's just you're young and got a little bit to learn yet."

Frye said, "Yes-sir."

"Now, Kirby, I want to remind you of something. We passed on your appointment as deputy. We could have gotten someone else, but we talked it over and decided you had the makings of a good one. Technically, you work for Danaher up in Tucson, but not if we hadn't passed on you. We used our judgment, Kirby . . . and our authority. Remember this, boy, as long as you're deputy you work for the people."

Frye said, "And all the people hung those two men?"

"A majority is all that's necessary," Stedman said.

"After you hung them," Frye asked quietly, "did you bury them?"

"Mendez took care of that," Beaudry said.

Frye looked at him. "Didn't your authority cover that?"

Tindal chuckled softly. "Kirby, now you're talking foolish."

Frye turned on him suddenly. "Doesn't killing two men mean anything to you?" He felt the anger hot on his face again.

Sundeen, sitting low in his chair, was fingering the chips in front of him. He said to no one in particular, "You picked yourself a beauty." He looked sideways at Jordan. "Why does he pack that gun if he's so against killin'?"

Jordan said, "Maybe it makes him feel important."

"Now if it was me," Sundeen said, "I wouldn't pick a deputy that whined like a woman."

Jordan was looking at Frye. "Maybe that's what this deputy is . . . only dressed up like a man."

Sundeen grinned. "Maybe we ought to take his pants off and find out."

Tindal chuckled. "Come on, Phil . . . don't be rough on him."

Frye held his eyes on Sundeen. Keep looking at him, just him, and don't let him think you're afraid. He's not an animal, he can't smell it, he has to use his eyes. Just Sundeen—he felt his anger mounting—and don't look at the other one, don't even think about him. He looks like he would fight with a gun, not with his fists, and you don't know anything about him. One thing at a time.

"Sundeen, if you want to try, stop by the jail tomorrow."

"Clay," Sundeen grinned, "did you hear what he said?"

Jordan was still looking at Frye. "Why would you wait till tomorrow?"

"That's what I was thinking," Sundeen said. He looked past Frye to Digo who still lounged in the doorway. "You hear what he said, Digo?"

Digo straightened. "I heard him."

"You think we should wait till tomorrow?"

"What for?"

Sundeen was grinning. "Can you do it alone?"

"Sure."

"All right. Get his pants off in two minutes and I'll buy you a drink."

"All the way off?"

"Just down."

Frye heard Digo behind him. Suddenly no more could be said because it was handed to Digo and Digo wasn't a talker, and with it there was hardly time to think about being afraid, only that you had to do something fast, without waiting.

He took a half step back turning, cocking his right fist, starting to swing at Digo who was almost on him, and Digo was seeing it, rolled head and shoulders out of the way. There it was. Frye shifted and jabbed his left fist hard into Digo's face. The face came up exposed for part of a second and Frye was ready. He swung hard with his right and Digo went back against the wall, his head striking the adobe next to the door frame. He started to go down, but he held himself against the wall and shook his head, clearing it and now wiping the blood from his mouth with the back of his hand.

Frye was on him again. He feinted, jabbed and swung, his fist landing solid against Digo's cheek, then the left, the right again, now to the stomach and a cross over to the face as Digo's guard dropped. Digo was covering, hunching his shoulders, but suddenly he swung.

His big fist came up from below grazing Frye's

chin, making him go back, and there was Digo's moment. Frye was open and Digo bore in, missing with his left but catching Frye's jaw with his right. Frye counterpunched with the ringing in his head, hitting Digo's face, but now Digo did not go back. An animal grunt came from him and he waded into Frye taking the stinging jabs, then swinging hard and now finding Frye's face with most of his blows. His guard went up and Digo's fist slammed into his stomach. Then the wall was behind him hard against his head, jolting his back, Digo swinging and the soft smacking sound of his fist against Frye's mouth. He tried to cover himself and Digo hammered through his guard, a grunting jab to the stomach. Frye's forearm went up for the blow to the head that would follow but it didn't come and again his body slammed against the wall as Digo went after his stomach.

He swung right and left backing Digo off, but only for a moment. Digo came again, taking jabs to the face and body as he closed in. He swung once, grazing Frye's head but his follow through was hard against Frye's cheekbone sending him back off balance. He kept after him until Frye was against the wall again and then he swung with every pound of his body behind it. Frye started to go down, but Digo held him by the front of his shirt and hit him again and again and again and each time he did Frye's head slammed against the adobe wall.

"That's enough, Digo!" Tindal screamed.

Digo let him fall. He backed away breathing hard, wiping his mouth. "He needs only twenty more pounds," Digo grunted, "and it could have been the other way."

Sundeen said, "You didn't do it."

Digo looked at him. "More than two minutes?"

Sundeen nodded. "But take his pants off anyway."

It was well after midnight when the wagon rolled into the street and stopped in front of the Metropolitan Café. Light framed the painted windows of De Spain's, but now there were no sounds from inside and across the street the windows of the jail office were dark. The street was silent, though the crickets could be heard if you listened for them.

Haig Hanasian climbed off the wagon seat and for a moment disappeared into the deeper shadow at the door of his café. He unlocked the door and returned unhurriedly to the wagon and close to the sideboard he said, "All right, come this way."

A man rose to his hands and knees in the wagon bed. He hesitated, then dropped silently over the sideboard of the wagon and as he did, two figures rose slowly, cautiously and followed him over the side. Haig Hanasian held open the door and they passed by him into the darkness of the café.

They stopped as he closed the door. "Be very

quiet," he said. "The tables are just to your left all the way to the back. The counter stools are along the right. Walk straight and you will not bump anything." He moved past them and they followed his steps to the kitchen. They heard him close the door. A match flared in the darkness and Haig lighted the lamp that was above the serving table.

The three men, who were in range clothes and watched Haig with full-open shifting eyes in dirt-streaked faces, were the men Sundeen had forced out of town. Merl White and the two Sun-D riders who had sided with him.

Haig said, "Sit down," glancing at them and then at the smaller table against the wall, then at their swollen bare feet, the shreds of wool socks and the traces of blood on the floor as they moved to the table. Haig pulled the chairs out for them. He began clearing the few soiled dishes from the table, but hesitated as he picked up the plate with the brown paper cigarette mashed in it. He put these dishes on the serving table, then went to the stove.

Merl White said, "What about your horses out front?"

"They are patient," Haig answered. He was a short heavy-set man and he spoke quietly, as if he were tired, and the heavy mustache over his mouth covered the movement of his lips.

"If you want to tend them," Merl White said, "I'll see to the fire."

"It's all right," Haig said, looking at Merl. But then his eyes went to the serving table, to the cigarette mashed out on the plate. He lighted the fire and moved the iron pot that was on the stove over the well. "It will be ready soon." He walked to the rear door that opened to the backyard. "I'll be gone only a few minutes," he said.

The three men were watching him. Merl said quickly, "Where're you going?"

Haig turned. "Don't you trust me?"

Merl swallowed. "I'm sorry . . . I guess we're edgy. We wondered what you planned."

"When I come back we will talk about it," Haig said.

"A man can't go far without boots."

Haig nodded. "We will talk about that, too."

He went outside, then up the back stairs to the second floor porch and through a door which opened to a hallway and just inside the door he lighted a table lamp. At the end of the hallway the living room was dark. Haig opened the door on the left, the door to his wife's bedroom, but he did not go in.

The room was dark, but the light from the hall fell across the bed and he could see her form under the comforter. She was lying on her side with her back toward him as he stood in the doorway and she did not move.

"Are you awake?"

"I am now," Edith said drowsily. Still she did not turn.

"I have to tell you something." She did not answer and he repeated, "Edith, I have to tell you something very important." He moved into the room and stood by the bed.

"What is it?"

"Those three men that were chased out of town—they're downstairs."

He expected his wife to look at him now, but she did not. "Did you wake me up to tell me that?"

"It concerns you," Haig said, "because they will be here until Monday night."

"Then what?"

"Then I'll take them to La Noria."

"The good Samaritan."

"I only ask that you stop entertaining Mr. Sundeen as long as they are here." Haig said this quietly, without emotion, as he had said all the things before.

She turned now, but only her shoulders and head on the pillow, her body twisted beneath the comforter and now the faint light showed her eyes and the outline of her features.

"I'll try," she said, beginning to smile.

"He was here this evening," Haig said.

"How would you know that?"

"He ate supper in the kitchen and you had coffee with him while he ate."

Now she recalled Kirby Frye, picturing him sitting across the table from her, but she said, "I didn't know watching someone eat was a sin."

"With you," Haig said, "it could be a very near occasion to it."

"You're absolutely sure Phil was here?"

"Who else?"

Edith rolled over lazily and with her back to him again said, "Imagine whatever you like."

5

Danaher came Sunday morning. He had been to La Noria on county business and had planned to stay there over Sunday before returning to Tucson, but two men rode in late Saturday afternoon with the story of the hanging at Randado and that changed Danaher's plans.

He left for Randado before sunup and all the way there he thought of Kirby Frye and wondered if he had returned. The two men told that the regular deputy had not been there, only the jailer.

And if Frye had returned, what?

Danaher had confidence in his deputy, though he kept reminding himself of it, because picturing Frye he saw a young man who looked too easygoing, who maybe smiled too readily and who called almost anyone older than himself mister. No, those things didn't matter, Danaher reminded himself. His confidence was based on a feeling and he relied on it more than he did the external evidences. A man could look like a lot of things, but Danaher let his intuition tell him what was beneath the surface.

A good deal of the time, Danaher felt alone in his job, this being sheriff of Pima County, and he liked to think that sometimes God gave him extra help—an above-natural power that allowed him to rely on his intuition in appraising people—a compensation for the loneliness of his job, and to make up for the minimum of help he could usually expect from others.

His intuition told him many things about Frye. That he was sensitive without being emotional, that he was respectful without being servile, and that he was a man who would follow what his conscience told him ninety-nine per cent of the time. That was the quality which sold Danaher, because he was sure he could make many of his own principles a part of that conscience, and in time he would have a real deputy. He showed Frye that he himself was a man to whom principle was everything and this way, whether Frye was aware of it or not, he won Frye's respect.

At the same time, Danaher was honest enough to admit to himself that maintaining Frye's respect would even make John Danaher a better man and he thought: That's how God tricks you into being good.

It hadn't taken long for him to like Frye, and that happened with few people he ever met. He respected him as a man, and with Danaher respect was something to be given out sparingly and only after substantial proof that it was deserved. Once he caught himself pretending that Kirby Frye was his son and he called himself a damn fool; but when he did it again he thought: Well, what's so unnatural about that? But the next time he saw Frye he spoke little and he bawled hell out of him for letting cigarette butts collect on the jail floor.

The first time he ever laid eyes on Frye was at Galluro Station the day after the Chiricahuas hit—

Danaher received the wire on a Saturday afternoon, from Fort Huachuca, relayed through the Benson operator. BRING POSSE GALLURO STATION HATCH AND HODGES LINE URGENT CHIRICAHUAS.

They reached Galluro Monday before noon, Danaher and eight men, only eight because raising a posse on Saturday wasn't the easiest thing in the world. They moved along at a steady but slower pace keeping their eyes open on the chance they might be riding into the running Chiricahuas and that was why it took them until Monday to get there.

The station had been partially burned, the stable and outbuildings, everything that wasn't adobe, and the teams had been run off. The dead were buried: the station agent and his wife and the Mexican hostler. But two people were missing: the hostler's wife and the little girl, and it was naturally assumed the Apaches had taken them. The agent's

wife had been in her forties, that was why she had
not been taken.

A Lieutenant J. R. Davis told them this.

He was there from Fort Huachuca with half of a
company, about eighteen men counting his Coyotero scout, plus two civilians who stood with their
thumbs in their belts waiting for something to happen. The other half of the company had gone out
the day before while the sign was still fresh, Lieutenant Davis told them; but he had waited in order
to tell Danaher their plan, which was no plan at all,
but the only alternative Davis could think of.

So, the first half of the company was to stay on
the sign as long as possible, following wherever it
led. Davis would take the remainder of the company and angle east by southeast for the Dragoons,
which was the logical place the Apaches would try
to reach no matter what direction they took from
Galluro. By Wednesday, Davis said, he hoped to
have made contact with the rest of the company by
heliograph. And if luck was with them, the
Apaches would be somewhere in between their
sun-flash messages.

Danaher was told to take his men west, back toward the Santa Catalinas, the way they had come,
and keep a sharp eye, because perhaps these
Apaches weren't heading for the Dragoons at all,
but trying to get away in a westerly direction.
Danaher was angry, because he could see the lieu-

tenant didn't believe this, but only said it because he had come all that way from Tucson with eight men and it was a shame not to have him doing something.

"How many were there?" Danaher asked.

"Not more than a dozen," Lieutenant Davis told him, and glanced at his scout. "That's what Dandy Jim reads."

"And you're pretty sure," Danaher said, "you can handle these twelve Chiricahuas by yourself."

"What do you mean?"

"Well, you're sending us off for home now you don't need us."

The lieutenant's face reddened, but it was anger and not embarrassment. "What do you mean don't need you? Couldn't they just as easily have gone toward the Catalinas?"

"You're not even considering it."

"My God, I can't go all four directions with eighteen men!"

Danaher felt sorry for him momentarily. The lieutenant had problems of his own to live with and to him they were bigger than anyone else's. There was no sense in aggravating him further. It wasn't the lieutenant's fault Danaher had been brought here; still, the Pima sheriff couldn't help one more small jab and he said, "Well, Lieutenant, how do you suppose I'm going to watch your western frontier with only eight men?"

The lieutenant's face was still flushed and he said angrily, "How many men would you like, Mr. Danaher?"

"Many as I can get."

"Will two be enough?"

"If that's all you can spare."

Davis motioned to the two civilians who were standing with Dandy Jim. "You men go with the sheriff here."

One of the men said, "You're orderin' the wrong boy. When I start ridin' it's back toward Huachuca."

Davis looked at the other man, scowling. "What about you?"

He was standing hip-shot with his thumbs in his belt and he nodded. "All right with me."

The first man said, "Kirby, what you want to go way over there for?"

"Well, Frank, our deal's closed, I thought I'd go on up to Prescott and visit with my folks."

Davis said, "Mr. Danaher, you get one man."

"That'll have to do then," Danaher said.

He glanced at the man who was coming with him, but did not take a second look because there wasn't anything out of the ordinary about him—though maybe he was lankier and lazier looking than the next man—and Danaher didn't bother to shake hands with him, but turned to his eight men and told them they would eat before starting back.

Then, drinking his coffee, Danaher looked over at Davis' half-of-a-company preparing to leave and he saw his new man and Davis' Coyotero scout squatting, talking together, and Danaher's interest advanced one step.

But it was not until later that he spoke to him. They had been riding for more than an hour and it came when the two of them happened to be riding side by side.

"What did that Coyotero tell you?" Danaher's first words.

"To stay awake."

Danaher looked at him because the boy's voice was calm and he had not been startled by the sheriff's abrupt question. "What do they call you?" Danaher said now.

"Frye."

"Frye what?"

"Kirby Frye."

"Where're you from?"

"Randado originally."

"Is that so? What else did that Coyotero say?"

"That maybe part of them went this way."

"What do you think?"

"I think he could be right."

Danaher half smiled. "Don't go out on a limb."

Frye glanced at him, saying nothing.

Danaher asked, "Did he tell the soldier that?"

"No."

"Why not?"

"It wouldn't make any difference with the few men he's got."

"Davis thought they'd run for the Dragoons," Danaher said.

"Well, he's probably right."

"So they could have gone either way and both Davis and the Coyotero are probably right."

"I'm saying," Frye said, "they could have gone *both* ways. Any Chiricahua could dodge soldier patrols and get back to the Dragoons, but he'd stop and give it some thought if he was driving those stage horses."

"So maybe the ones with the horses went this way," Danaher concluded.

"That's right."

"But if they were to drive them west, then make a long swing back to the Dragoons, that would take time."

"They've got more of it than anybody else," Frye said.

They camped without a fire on flat ground, but with foothills looming in the near distance. It was the boy, Kirby Frye, who suggested no fire. The men grumbled because as far as they were concerned they were going home, not stalking hostiles; but Danaher agreed with Frye and said bluntly, flatly, no fire, and that's all there was to it. They ate jerked beef and biscuits, then lay on their stomachs to smoke, holding the glow cupped close to the ground. One man, with a cigarette in his mouth, stood up and walked off a few feet to relieve himself. He turned, surprised, seeing Danaher next to him, but had no time to dodge as Danaher's fist swung against his jaw. Without a word Danaher stepped on the cigarette and returned to the circle of his possemen.

In the morning as soon as they reached high ground, they saw the dust. Far off beyond the sweep of the grade below them, hanging clear and almost motionless in the distance, seeming only a few hundred yards off in the dry air but at least four hours ahead of them, beyond arroyos and cutbanks that were only shadow lines in their vision. Horses raised dust like that and every man there knew it. And when they moved on, down the sweep of the grade, there was an excitement inside of them that wasn't there before. Danaher could feel it and he knew the others did, but they rode loose and kept it inside and tried to look as if this was something they did every other day of the week.

Well, Danaher thought, watching his men when they weren't watching him, that was a good sign. They're good men and maybe I shouldn't have hit that one last night. Now they know they're not just riding home and they'll act like grown men.

But later on Danaher's men let their excitement

show. Since noon they had been deep among the hills, winding through the shadows of brush and rock formations, moving single file with two men a mile or so ahead, moving slowly but gaining steadily on the column of dust which they would see only occasionally now.

About two o'clock they heard rifle fire up ahead and soon after one of Danaher's advance riders was coming back. They could read good news all over his face.

Danaher side-stepped his big chestnut gelding to block the trail and the rider came up short, almost swinging out of the saddle. He had been yelling something as he rode in and now Danaher told him to shut up and take a breath and they'd find out what happened a lot quicker.

"Now what's it all about?"

"John, we *got* one!"

The man's name was Walt Booth and he was the same one who had showed his cigarette glow the night before and Danaher had hit. He was quick tempered and easily roused to fight, but Danaher could handle him and that's why he always let Booth join the posses.

Now Booth told them what had happened. How they had topped a rise and there right below them, but beyond a brush thicket, were eight or ten horses in a clearing like they'd been held up to rest.

It hit them right away, Booth told. Stage teams from Galluro! And that meant only one thing—

"We started to rein around and I heard it. A snappin' sound in the brush. Now I had my piece across my lap and my finger on the trigger—had it there all morning—and I'm broadside to the thicket when I hear the noise and the next second this son-of-a-bitchin' 'Pache's standin' there gawkin' at me. He starts to run, but he's a split-haired second late and I let him catch it right between the wings." Booth was grinning. "Didn't even have to lift the piece, just squeezed one off and he flops over like a sack of fresh cow chips."

Danaher asked him how many Apaches, but Booth didn't know. When he fired the horses started to move, just like that, like a signal, and they didn't see even one, though they fired at the horses because you know how the bastards cling to the off side of a mount and make you think there're no riders while all the time they're ridin' the hell out.

He told that the other advance man was watching the place and they'd better shake their tails up there if they were going to have 'Pache for dinner.

Danaher let Booth go first, then told the others to follow and he swore if a man made a sound he'd break him in two. But their excitement was up again and they did make sounds in the loose shale and brushing through mesquite and all Danaher could do was swear to himself.

The other advance rider was not in sight, but they found the dead Apache right away. Booth said damned if he oughtn't to lift the greasy scalp . . . show his wife he was really out here . . . but Danaher told him to keep away. Frye came up to him then. He watched Frye kneel over the dead Apache and heard him say something about the Apache being only a boy. Not over fourteen.

Well, that was too bad. Danaher had live Apaches to think about. He directed his men to the clearing where the horses had been and when they got there the other advance man who had been with Booth was coming out of the brush on the other side. He was running and pointing behind him.

"John, they're runnin' like blue hell down a draw!"

"How many?"

"Not a mile ahead! John, we got 'em runnin' for the open!"

"How many!"

The man reached them and he stopped, breathing heavily. "I didn't see 'em . . . I heard 'em! This draw's full of scrub pine—must slant down two miles before she opens up. Way off over the trees you can see open country where the draw comes out. And all the time I could hear the red sons beatin' down through the trees!"

"But you didn't see them come out," Danaher said.

"Settin' there was time wasted. I came back to get you."

Danaher swung up over his saddle and went through the brush at a gallop. The others followed. They topped the knoll that formed the beginning of the draw, listening and hearing nothing, but seeing off in the distance, below and off beyond the slanting brown-green smooth-appearing tops of the scrub pines, the dust trail. Dust that was rising thinly to nothing and pinpoint dots inching into the wide open flat glare of the distance. Booth said, "We're going to have us a late supper, but damn' if it won't be worth it."

Danaher was ready and he turned in the saddle to make sure that his men were. This is what they had come for and by God they'd run the Apaches till they caught them. His men were ready, sitting their mounts eagerly. All of them except the boy, Kirby Frye.

He was standing in front of his horse, holding the reins close to the bit rings and gazing up at the wild brush and rocks that followed a looming jog back off to the left of them.

Danaher asked, "You coming?"

Frye's gaze swung to Danaher. "I don't know about chasing after that dust."

"What do you mean?"

"It doesn't seem right they'd be running for open country."

One of the men said, "John, we got to move!"

Danaher scowled. "Hold on!" And to Frye, "Make some sense."

"I never heard of an Apache getting himself caught out on flat land. They mostly camp high, even if it's a dry camp, and *always* if somebody's on their sign."

Danaher said, "But if we surprised them they didn't have a choice but to streak for the best opening."

Frye shook his head. "I never heard of a Chiricahua raiding party being even approached without their knowing about it."

"That 'Pache over yonder," Booth sneered, "sure'n hell opened a surprise package when he stuck his head out the bushes." Booth's eyes held on Frye. "Who says you know so goddamn much about 'Paches? That stuff last night about no fire—"

"The one you got was a boy," Frye interrupted. "He hadn't yet learned the finer points."

Booth glanced at the rider next to him. "He's a goddamn Indin lover. Chief No-Fire." He looked back to Frye. "Chief No-Fire-In-His-Pants. Let me ask you a question, Chief. Are you tellin' us this 'cause you're an Indin lover or 'cause you're too goddamn scared to go down that draw?"

Danaher almost interrupted, but he glanced at Frye and suddenly checked himself. The boy hadn't moved, hadn't flickered his eyes from Booth's face. Booth was almost broadside to him, the Remington rolling, block across his lap, and pointed just off from Frye, and the boy still held his reins short, but his right hand was at his side now, thumb almost touching the hickory butt of his Colt.

Frye said, "Mister, were you asking a question, or telling me a fact?" Booth had been leaning over the saddle horn, but now he straightened slowly and the barrel of the Remington edged a wavering inch toward Frye.

"Take it any way you want," Booth said.

"If it wasn't a question," Frye said, "then you better start doin' something with that Remington."

"Hold on!" Danaher broke in. He had been intrigued by the boy's calmness, by the way Frye stared back at a rifle barrel almost on him and dumped the play back into the other man's lap; but it had to end. And Danaher was the man to end it.

"Time's wasting." He glared at Frye. "Get it out, quick. Why don't you think it's them? Even though you can see their dust."

"We make dust just like they do," Frye said. "I'll judge they sent a man back to look us over sometime yesterday afternoon."

"Go on."

"They decided we were getting too close, so the

thing to do was throw us off. It was either keeping their skins or the horses. Their skins got the vote and the horses were elected to side-track us. That's what you see down there, the Hatch and the Hodges Stage horses they took from Galluro."

Danaher said, "And you think the braves are up here in the rocks somewhere."

Frye nodded.

"That boy getting shot," Danaher said. "Was that part of the side-tracking?"

A few of his men laughed, Booth one of them.

"That's the way they learn," Frye said. "They either graduate or get dropped out of school suddenly."

"What else?" Danaher said.

"The rest is guess."

"Go ahead."

"There were three boys and one warrior, the instructor you might say. Probably this run on Galluro was the first raid they've taken part in. They were to just take care of the horses and get them back home somehow. Now there weren't enough for an ambush and we were too close to be outrun, so they had only one thing left to do. Throw us off and get the hell home."

"You admit that's a guess," Danaher said.

"Most of it. I wasn't there when they talked it over."

Danaher shook his head. "That dust over there is

something we can see. Maybe they're only horses as you say, but it's something there and you don't have to guess to know it."

Frye nodded. "Yes sir. You coming back this way?"

Danaher looked at him. "You mean you're going to stay here?"

"They come back for their dead when they can."

"That's presupposing quite a bit."

Frye shrugged. "When you come back I'll ride on to Tucson with you."

Danaher hesitated. There were words he could use to cut a fresh know-it-all kid down to manageable size. Words almost in his mouth. But he hesitated. The way the boy said it wasn't cheeky or show-off; it was perhaps just the words themselves, if you took them alone. So he hesitated because he was unsure and later on he was glad that he did.

He took his men down the draw, down through the scrub pine to the plain and pointed them into the distance, ran them until mounts and men were salt- and sweat-caked, halted them for the sake of the horses not the men, moved them again, gaining on the dust cloud, now making out pinpoint dots again, drawing closer, closer, until finally—there it was.

He drew up his posse and sat heavily, silently watching the riderless Hatch and Hodges Line stage horses streak into the distance again.

And all the way back to the draw, in the approaching dusk, he was silent. He was not angry because he had made a mistake. He did not expect to be right all the time. This was even a justifiable miscalculation for that matter. A bird in the hand always and any way you looked at it being worth more than the two in the bush. Well, maybe not always. He was thinking of Kirby Frye and the matter-of-fact way he had read the situation. No, the one in the hand isn't always the best. Not if somebody tells you the bush is right under your nose and all you have to do is stick your hand in.

Reaching the top of the draw Danaher was thinking: But he better not say, "I told you so."

Moving into the clearing he expected to see Frye get up and watch them ride in. Wasn't that him lying over there? It was in his mind and at the same moment Booth, swinging down next to him, answered the question.

"That's the 'Pache I shot!"

The Apache boy had been left in the brush, but now, strangely, he was near the edge of the clearing. And still Frye was not in sight.

"John, there's a note on him."

"What?"

"Right on his chest, a rock weightin' it down!" Booth looked at it, even though he couldn't read, before handing it to Danaher.

It was a yellow sheet of paper that had been

folded twice but was now open and the side he looked at was a receipt form with the information that thirty-three cavalry remounts had been delivered and—

Danaher turned the paper between his fingers. Frye's message was on the other side, written in pencil.

Don't move the dead one. 35 paces off his right shoulder in the brush is a wounded Cherry-cow. Gutshot. Don't give him water. Will see you by dark.

And the last line: *Horses run like hell without saddles, don't they?*

One thought struck Danaher at that moment. It had been building in him since meeting Frye, evolving slowly as Frye, step by step, advanced in Danaher's estimation; first, seeing him talking to the Coyotero tracker; then last night, he was the one who had suggested no fire; then the way he stood up to Booth's nervous Remington with ice water in his eyes and a voice like he was asking the time of day; and the fact that he had read this Apache scheme like words on a printed page.

He'd make one hell of a fine deputy, was Danaher's thought. And he realized now that perhaps he had been thinking it, or half wishing it, all the time.

The note clinched it in Danaher's mind. He carries a pencil! Maybe he can't spell Chiricahua, but by God "Cherry-cow" was close enough and all the rest of the words were right.

He was still thinking about this when Kirby Frye returned. He came out of the brush and was next to Danaher before the sheriff realized he was there.

"Where've you been?"

"After the other two."

So he was right, Danaher thought. Four altogether. "You get them?"

"One. The other disappeared."

In the almost dark Danaher studied him. "Probably the older brave."

"I never got close enough to tell."

"Why'd they come back?"

"To pick up the dead one. They thought we'd all gone."

"Well, three dead out of four isn't bad."

Frye looked at Danaher anxiously. "The one I hit in the belly's dead?"

"Booth finished him." Danaher asked then, "Why didn't you?"

"I didn't create him," Frye answered. "I don't see where I had a right to uncreate him."

"What about the other one? You killed him."

"Not when he was lying on the ground gutshot."

"What's the difference?"

Frye hesitated. "Mr. Danaher, don't you see a difference?"

He did, but he wasn't going to stand in a mesquite

thicket all night discussing Apache-country ethics, so he said, "Maybe we'll talk about it over a beer sometime."

And he was thinking: No question of it now. He's my man.

After they reached Tucson he asked Frye if he'd mind stopping by the jail. Danaher relaxed a little and smiled to himself when Frye said yes sir, he'd be happy to. Might even buy the boy a drink, he decided, after they had something to eat.

And later, after tacos and a glass of beer, now sitting in the jail office, Danaher with his back to the roll-top, Frye appearing comfortable slouched in a Douglas chair, both smoking cigarettes—

"I'd like to ask you a few things," Danaher began.

"Go ahead."

"There's a reason."

Frye shrugged. "I figured there was."

"Well . . . you said you were from Randado."

"Originally."

"How long ago?"

Frye looked at the beamed ceiling, then at Danaher. "I was born there. My dad was a mining man then and felt he ought to work the Huachucas. So we lived in Randado while he prospected."

"And how long did you stay?"

"I left the first time when I was fourteen."

"For where?"

"With a trail herd."

"Old man Sundeen's?"

Frye nodded. "Yes sir. That was before Willcox became a pickup point for the railroad. We drove them all the way to Ellsworth."

"I imagine you learned a few things on Douglas Street," Danaher said seriously.

Frye grinned. "A few things."

"And then what?"

"The next year we drove part of the herd to McDowell and the rest over to San Carlos and Old Val sold them all as government beef for the reservation."

"Go on."

"Well, I didn't go back with them that trip, but stayed on at San Carlos and worked for the agent a while."

"And that's where you learned about Apaches."

"I learned some."

"I guess you did."

"That same year my folks moved up to Prescott and my dad started a freight line with what he'd scratched out of the Huachucas."

"He sounds like the one prospector in a thousand," Danaher observed, "with some sense."

"All he wanted was enough to start a business with," Frye explained.

"That's what they all say."

"Well, my dad was always good for his word."

"You favor him?"

"I don't know . . . they always said I favored my mother. She was from right here in Tucson. One of the Kirby girls . . . her dad was a lawyer, W. F. Kirby?"

"I've only been here for a few years," Danaher said. "What did you do, work for your dad?"

"Yes sir. I drove one of his freight wagons."

"Did you help him keep books?"

"Some."

"Your mother saw that coming when she taught you to read and write."

Frye looked at him surprised. "How'd you know that?"

"You don't talk like you came out of the hills, but you haven't had time to go to school. Which did you get tired of first," he said then, "the freight wagon or the ledger?"

"You sure know a lot about me."

"You left, didn't you?"

"Yes sir. I went to work for a man supplying remounts to the cavalry."

"How long did you do that?"

"For him, a couple of years."

"Then you went in business for yourself."

He frowned, the frown changing to a grin as Frye shook his head. "I don't know why I'm doing any talking."

"Did you work alone?"

"I had two Coyotero boys."

"And they taught you a little more."

"A lot more."

"Where'd you sell?"

"Huachuca mostly. I'd just sold a string of bang-tails there when Davis said he was going to Galluro and asked did we want to come along."

"Was that tracker of his one of your boys?"

"Dandy Jim? No, he works just for the Fifth Cavalry. My boys quit on the trip before that one, so I took on a partner."

"The one who was with you at Galluro."

"Yes sir. But he didn't like to work much. I was glad when he said no about going with you; that gave me a chance to break our partnership. It was just on a trial."

Danaher was silent. Finally he said, "Then you haven't been back to Randado in about ten years."

"That's right."

"You remember Old Val Sundeen."

"Yes sir."

"And his boy?"

"I remember him. He was about six years older than me then."

"Phil."

"That's right, Phil."

"Did you get along with him?"

"Well—"

"Not too good, uh?"

"Not too."

"Phil's running the spread now. Old Val's got something eating at his insides and he hardly gets out of bed."

Frye said, "That's too bad," frowning.

"You remember R. D. Tindal?"

"I remember Mr. Tindal. He had a girl, Milmary."

"He still does. You remember Beaudry?"

"The name's familiar."

"What about Harold Mendez?"

Frye shook his head. "I don't think so."

"Harold's deputy at Randado, but he's quitting."

"Oh."

"Do you want his job?"

"What does it pay?"

Danaher had expected him to hesitate. He stared at Frye slouched comfortably in the chair returning his gaze calmly. "Seventy-five a month," Danaher answered, "plus a dollar for each drunk and disorderly arrest. You get something else if you have to collect taxes. I suppose it's less than you might make trading horses, but it's steadier. Do you want the job?"

Frye straightened in the chair and said, "I think it'd be fine." Just like that.

You can't be sure, Danaher told himself now, dismounting in front of the Randado jail. Even with

Godgiven intuition you can't always judge a man quickly. He told himself that because Frye was only twenty-four and because, more than anything else, he didn't want to be wrong about him.

6

of the soldiers?"

"I'm sorry you have to be kept in this cell," Frye said to Dandy Jim, who stood close to him but seemed to be farther away because of the heavy iron bars that separated them. He hesitated. "Listen," he went on, speaking to the Coyotero in Spanish, "I could leave this door open if it would make a difference to you."

The Coyotero seemed to consider this. "Why would it make a difference," he said then, "knowing I must remain here?"

"I promised the soldier in charge that I would hold you until he returned," Frye explained.

Dandy Jim said nothing. He could not understand this and that was the reason he did not speak; and he was not sure if it would be proper to ask why the soldiers had the right to hold him or request of another that he be held. And at the same time, looking at Frye, he tried not to notice his swollen mouth, the bruises on both cheek bones and the left eye which was purple-blue and almost closed. He knew it would not be proper to ask about his disfigurement. Perhaps, though, he could ask about the other since he had known this man many years—

"Tell me," he said, suddenly having decided to ask it, "why is what I did to that woman a concern of the soldiers?"

"I don't understand," Frye answered.

"It was my woman, I found her with another, this Susto if you know him, and did what I had to do."

"When was that?"

"Just before the soldiers came."

Frye was silent. Then, "After you disfigured her you drank the tulapai?"

Dandy Jim nodded.

"With others, and perhaps you made noise?"

"Perhaps."

"To be overheard by someone who might tell the soldiers if it meant a reward?"

"That might be."

"Well, that's why they chased you . . . the tulapai, not because of what you did to your wife." Watching Dandy Jim, Frye could see that this explanation did not seem reasonable to him, so he said, "I'll tell you, without wasting words, that when the Apache drinks tulapai, the soldiers are afraid. That's their reason for taking it away from you."

Dandy Jim said, "When the soldiers drink aguardiente, who takes that from them?"

"No one."

"Is no one afraid of them?"

"Some are, but in a way that is different."

Dandy Jim could not reasonably carry this further, so he said, "Then that about my woman has nothing to do with why I am here."

"I'm almost certain it does not." Frye asked then, "Do you need tobacco?" And when the Coyotero shook his head, he said, "I'll come back again to talk to you."

And when he was gone Dandy Jim thought and continued to think that even this white man whom he had known so many years, even him he did not understand. Something made the white men different from Apache and he did not know what it was. Yes, even this one who could do many things which were Apache, even he was different when you closed your eyes and thought about him, remembering the small things he said which were not really small but kept small because they were things that could not be explained. Like this tulapai thing. He said that soldiers were afraid of the Apache who drank tulapai. That was keeping it simple and small.

And probably he does not approve of what I did to the woman, even though he says I am not being held for that. But it was not his wife, and he did not see her through the willows lying with another man. Susto.

He thought about the woman again, though he had ceased calling her his wife.

It was the tulapai he had been drinking on the way home that brought the rage. He would not have done it sober. Beat her, yes; but not mutilate her. But even as he thought of it he was angry again. It was not his fault that he was gone most of the time as a tracker for the soldiers. Did she expect him to grow corn? He was a warrior and would fight either for the soldiers or against them and at this time it was not only more profitable, but wiser to fight for them. He was not asked to go against Coyoteros. Only Chiricahuas and sometimes Mimbreños, people he did not usually approve of under any circumstances. But he did it as much for her as for himself and that was what angered him. That while he was away, working to be able to buy cloth and beads as well as ammunition, she would lie with another man. Susto. Susto of all men. She had been a Lipan woman, taken on a raid, and perhaps he should never have trusted her.

No, he was sure Frye did not approve of his treatment of the woman, though this did not show on his face. There was their difference again.

When Frye first became known to him he seldom thought of this difference. That time at San Carlos. And the first day they spoke—

They were just beginning the foot race and the white boy came up to them and asked if he could take part. For weeks he had watched their games while they pretended that he was not watching, but this day he asked if he might join. And while laughing to themselves they told him, seriously, yes he could join them, but would he not like to make a wager? Say his horse? All of this was half in Spanish and half Apache and English and it took time.

Then, after he had put up his horse they told him that of course he knew this was not an ordinary foot race. Dandy Jim himself, Tloh-ka then, pointed, explaining that they would run following the bending course of that arroyo to the clump of mesquite part of the way up the hill ("You will know it by the way it claws at your face"), then back again, a distance of two and a half miles. And, of course, the contestants would be blindfolded, their hands tied behind them and would carry a knife, by the blade, between their teeth. Whoever did not return with a knife still in his mouth would forfeit his horse to the winner of the race. There was an old Coyotero man there to see that each boy abided by the rules which forbade attempting a short cut or trying to trip an opponent.

Twice that afternoon they ran the race and when it was over Kirby Frye still had his horse. He had not won any of the races, but he still had his horse. Later, years later, Dandy Jim learned Frye had been practicing this alone for weeks.

There were other games in those days at San

Carlos: Apache games, and in all of them Frye did well and in competing in the games there was never the thought that this boy was different from them, not after that first foot race. In time he even spoke some words of their language.

Thinking of those days now, it occurred to Dandy Jim, that, yes, they were different even then, because whatever it was that made them different was inside and must have been present from the moment of conception. It was just that they did not have the time then to notice it.

But he is a good man, Dandy Jim thought, and I think it would be a rare thing to track with him or go to war as his companion . . . to do something which would leave no time for thinking about this difference.

Danaher had been talking to Harold Mendez for almost a quarter of an hour when Frye came down the stairs. Time enough to learn how the hanging had taken place and to learn again that Frye had not been present; though he refrained from asking what Frye had done about it.

And now, seeing Frye's swollen face, it wasn't necessary to ask. He felt relief sag inside of him and he exhaled slowly, inaudibly, all of the tension that he had carried with him from La Noria. Frye had done something, there was no question about that.

"Kirby, you look a bit worse for wear," Danaher

said, sitting down and pointing with his eyes for Frye to sit down also. "How do you feel?"

"I don't know. I think all my front teeth are loose."

"Don't eat anything chewy for a while and they'll settle again. Who did it?"

"Sundeen's jinete."

"Digo the horsebreaker," Danaher said as if reflecting, picturing him. Then, "What are you going to do about it?"

"I don't know."

"What about Tindal and the others; what're you going to do about them?"

Frye seemed suddenly worn out and he only shrugged his shoulders.

Danaher was silent for a moment watching Frye. He told himself to take it easy or he'd lose a deputy. But no, the hell with that, if he wants to quit then let him get out now, out of the way. Baby him and you'll be holding his hand from now on, Danaher thought.

So he said, "How long are you going to sit here?"

"I don't know."

"You don't know very much, do you?"

Frye looked up. "What would you do?"

"I'd slap 'em with warrants."

"I don't know if I could do it."

Danaher said, "You've got a gun."

"I walk up to Tindal, and tell him he's under arrest, and if he objects I draw on him."

"You've got it fairly straight," Danaher said, "but I'll write it out if you want."

"John—" Frye hesitated; it was the first time he had called Danaher by his first name. It just popped out and momentarily he looked at Danaher as if expecting him to object, but there was no reaction from him, nothing on Danaher's face to indicate an objection. And Frye thought briefly, flashingly: You make a big thing out of everything. You make a problem out of whether you should use a first name or a mister . . . which was half the reason it didn't go right at De Spain's last night. You were being too respectful, so they shoved it down your throat.

"John," he repeated the name purposely. "Maybe I'm sitting here because I'm afraid. I'll get that out in the open first. But there's something else. Last night Tindal told me that I worked for Randado, that is, the people of Randado. And if the people of Randado elect to have a law their way, one that benefits them as a whole, then I have to go along with the people I serve."

Danaher nodded. "That sounds like Tindal. But there's one thing wrong with the statement. You work for me."

"I know I do, but these are the people right here I actually serve."

Danaher leaned forward in his chair. "Let me tell you something, if you don't already know it," he said quietly. "I'm paid pretty well to keep order in a stretch of land as big as any one man's been asked to watch. I've got people above me, but they give me a free hand; those were my terms. I'm the law here, Kirby. I've got a conscience and God to account to, but I'm the law and when I say something's wrong, it's wrong . . . until a higher authority proves otherwise." Danaher continued to look at Frye, holding him with his eyes.

"You said you might be scared. Well, I was boogered once, shaking in my boots making my first arrest of a wanted man. After that I took men with me because it was quicker and I no longer had to prove to myself, or to anybody else, I could do it. You proved yourself by standing up to them. Now get some men behind you and slap warrants on Tindal, Beaudry, Stedman, Sundeen and Digo—"

"What about Clay Jordan?" Frye said, because he thought of him suddenly as Danaher named the others and he wanted to see Danaher's reaction.

"Was he here?" Danaher's face showed nothing.

"They say he wasn't in on the hanging."

Danaher paused. "Then don't touch him."

"Do you know him?"

"I know him." Danaher rose saying this.

"He looks like a gun-tipper."

"Don't try to find out," Danaher said.

"I might have trouble getting men to back me," Frye said, "when I pass out the warrants."

"That's your problem. You get paid for figuring out things like that."

Frye's swollen lips formed a smile. "I'll try. But I can't promise anything."

That was all Danaher wanted to hear. He said, "Wire Tucson when you've served them. If I don't hear from you by Wednesday I'll come back."

Frye nodded, but said, "How do you know I won't quit?"

"Kirby," Danaher answered, "I just have to look at your busted face."

7

"There must be a better way to do this," Harold Mendez said. He was watching Frye, who was sitting at the desk filling in the names on the warrants. The warrants already bore Judge Ira M. Finnerty's illegible scrawl in the lower right corner, which to Frye always seemed proof enough of Danaher's influence—anyone who could get Judge Finnerty to sign blank warrants that would be used sometime in the future—

"Maybe Danaher's right," Frye answered the jailer. "He'd throw them in jail and not make any bones about it."

"But you're not Danaher," Mendez said.

"I just don't think they have to be thrown in jail." The warrants would be served, but instead of jailing them they would be ordered not to leave the vicinity between now and the next court date scheduled for December 18, three weeks away. And since their families and businesses were here Frye decided it wouldn't be necessary for them to post bond. But it will be hard living with them, he thought. Then Judge Finnerty will decide to hold the hearing at Tucson and that will make it all the worse, making them ride eighty-five miles for their comeuppance.

Sunday, the day before, he did not see any of them. He came to the jail in the morning to relieve Harold and to talk to Dandy Jim; but after Danaher left he went back to his room—a boardinghouse down the street—and stayed there through most of the afternoon and evening, not even visiting De Spain's after supper. Let them cool off. Sunday might have a soothing effect on them and it would be easier Monday when he served the warrants.

"Harold, maybe you could find out if Beaudry's about while I visit Tindal and Stedman."

"All right," Harold nodded. "What about Sundeen?"

"I'll go out there about suppertime."

"When his whole crew's in," Harold added.

"I have to serve Digo, too," Frye answered. He left the jail, slipping the warrants into his inside coat pocket, and walked along the shade of wooden awnings to the Randado branch of the Cattlemen's Bank. He glanced across the street to Tindal's store before going inside and he thought of Milmary as he approached the railed-off section of the bank's office.

"Louise, could I see Mr. Stedman?"

The blond girl at the front desk looked up. "He isn't in," she said stiffly.

"Where would he be?"

"I don't know."

"No idea?"

"Maybe he's at dinner."

"It's a little early for that."

"Mr. Stedman doesn't tell me everything he does."

"All right." Frye started to go. "You might tell him I was here."

"Don't worry," the girl said after him.

He crossed the street to Tindal's. Opening the door and closing it with the jingling of the bell, he saw Milmary behind the counter. She was facing the shelves, a writing board in her arm, and Frye knew that she had seen him. She would have turned hearing a customer.

"Mil—"

"Just leave your warrant on the counter and get out of here."

He hesitated. "How do you know I have a warrant?"

"Everybody in town saw Danaher yesterday. Why else would you be here?"

Now it was out in the open and that made it simpler, if nothing else. "I'm looking for your dad."

"I don't know where he is."

"Maybe he's having dinner with Mr. Stedman."

"Why don't you"—she turned suddenly, hesitating as she saw his bruised face, and though her tone was softer she finished—"look for him. Isn't that what they pay you for, looking for criminals?"

"I thought you might save me some steps," Frye said. "Maybe he's at home."

"Maybe he is," Milmary said.

"Or at De Spain's?"

"Or in Mexico! Why don't you just leave?"

"All right, Mil."

"Kirby—"

He was turning to go and now he looked back at her. "What?"

"Who did that to you?" She nodded gently, almost frowning.

"Digo," Frye answered. He hesitated, still looking at her, but slowly her eyes dropped from his. He turned then and left.

Harold Mendez was at the window when Frye opened the door. He nodded to a line of Sun-D horses hitched in front of De Spain's and said, "They came while you were at Tindal's. It looked funny because as you were coming out they were going into De Spain's."

"Is Phil there?"

"Phil and Digo and Jordan and three or four

more." Harold's eyes went to the line of horses and he said, "That's right, seven of them."

"I didn't even hear them," Frye said.

"You were thinking of something else," Harold said. He saw Frye look at the rifle rack and then at the desk, then walk over to the desk, not sitting down but only touching it with his fingers, then come over to the window and Harold was thinking: I'm glad I'm not in his shoes; and said, "Did you serve the warrants?"

"Neither one of them were there."

"Something funny's going on," Harold said. "Wordie Stedman was passing and I asked him if he'd seen Mr. Beaudry, but he went right on without stopping."

"He might have had something to do."

"Didn't even look back."

"Well, I don't know—"

"Kirby, the word's out on this warrant business and nobody likes it. That's what it is."

Frye nodded slowly, looking across the street. "It didn't take long for them to find out, did it?"

"They saw Danaher and they know Danaher wouldn't fool around," Harold said. "You know they can make it hard for you to serve those warrants."

"I don't understand that, Harold. Everybody wasn't in on the hanging. Why should they stick up for the few that were?"

Harold shrugged. "Maybe it's just that nobody likes Danaher. Or at least they feel closer to Tindal and Stedman . . . and Beaudry, and it's a matter of principle with them. Like helping out a kin who's in trouble. Not necessarily because you like him, but because he's a him."

Frye said, "Do they feel that way about Sundeen?"

"They don't have to worry about Sundeen. Listen," Harold went on, "probably everybody isn't against you." He hesitated. "But that isn't much consolation because it seems like everybody, doesn't it?"

Frye nodded.

"I know how you feel," Harold said. "I'm glad I don't have to feel that way any more. It's something that comes with the job but isn't important until something like this happens. You know I used to go out of my way to be nice to people . . . always with a good word; then one day I just got sick to my stomach of smiling, and I quit." Harold's eyes went to the window and he said abruptly, "There's Digo on the porch."

"I saw him," Frye said. He nodded. "He's going in again."

"What does that tell you?" Harold said.

Frye was silent, watching the front of De Spain's, and he was thinking: How long will it take? The tails of the horses switched lazily in the sunlight of the street, but the shade of the porch was deserted and nothing moved there.

"What did you say, Harold?" But now he wasn't listening and he knew Harold would not answer. He saw both doors of De Spain's swing open and hold open as they came out: Phil Sundeen first, Digo moving next to him as he started across the street; the one called Jordan was directly behind Sundeen and spreading out behind him were the four other Sun-D riders.

"Harold, unlock the rifles."

"You can't stop all of them."

"Before you do, go up and open Dandy Jim's cell."

"I'll give you a rifle first."

"No . . . get up there quick!"

Frye moved to the door and opened it. In the sunlight, halfway across the street, Sundeen hesitated. As Frye stepped into the doorway Sundeen came on again until less than twenty feet separated them. Digo came even with Sundeen, but Jordan stayed back. He was almost directly behind Sundeen.

Frye watched them, holding himself calm, knowing what would come, but not being sure what to do. They've rehearsed this, he thought, so let them play it.

"I hear," Sundeen called, "you got warrants to serve."

Frye hesitated. "That's right."

"You got one for me?"

Frye nodded.

"One for Digo?"

"That's right."

"What about the Committee?"

"For three of them."

"But they're not about."

Frye nodded again.

"What about Jordan?"

"None for that name."

Sundeen grinned. "None for Mr. Jordan. Why don't you have one for him?"

"He wasn't part of the hanging."

Sundeen stood relaxed. "I don't think that's the reason."

"I don't care what you think," Frye told him.

Sundeen glanced at Digo. "Listen to the boy sheriff."

Digo grinned, looking up from the cigarette he was shaping. "He's something."

"I think you're afraid to put his name on a warrant," Sundeen said. "That's the reason."

"You think whatever you like," Frye answered. Behind him he could hear Harold Mendez coming down the stairs.

Sundeen took a full step to the side, half turning, saying, "I don't believe you met Mr. Jordan."

"Not formally," Frye said.

"Mr. Jordan takes care of my legal affairs." Sundeen nodded to Jordan who was standing directly in line with Frye now, his coat open and his thumbs hooked close to the buckle of his gunbelt.

Frye said, "Then he can advise you about the warrant you're getting."

"He says I'm not going to get one. Digo either."

Now it's coming, Frye thought, holding himself still in the doorway, making himself relax. He didn't know what to say, so he kept his jaw clenched and his eyes steady on Sundeen.

"Jordan says I won't get one 'cause you're not man enough to serve it. He says when a sheriff's got a yellow streak then he's got no authority to serve warrants."

"Do you want it right now?" Frye asked.

"You can try," Sundeen grinned.

"But you'd rather see me try for my gun."

"You might just as well. If your hand went inside your coat how's Jordan to know whether it's for a warrant or a gun. He'd have to protect himself."

"What's he got to do with this?"

"I told you, he's my lawyer. Digo's too." Saying this he glanced at the Mexican. "That's right?"

"Nothing but the best," Digo said, taking the cigarette from his mouth.

"So if you got something to take out of your pocket," Sundeen added, "it's for Mr. Jordan."

Frye's gaze shifted to Jordan, then returned to Sundeen. He hesitated before saying, "You won't try to stop me because that would be resisting arrest, but there's no warrant for him and if I put a hand in my pocket he'll draw and you'll all swear he shot in self-defense . . ."

"This boy's a thinker," Sundeen said to Digo.

"That's if he shoots first," Frye added, and immediately, in the silence that followed, he was sorry he had said it.

Sundeen was grinning again as he turned to Jordan. "You hear what he said?"

Jordan's gaze remained on Frye. "I heard him." This was the first time he had spoken; his voice was calm and his eyes watched Frye almost indifferently though they did not leave him for a moment.

"He thinks he's faster than you are," Sundeen said.

"Maybe he is."

"Only one way to find out."

Jordan nodded, still looking at Frye. "Let's see those warrants."

"They're not for you."

"I didn't ask who they were for."

"I'll serve them when I'm ready."

Jordan nodded slowly. "How's your mother?"

"What?"

"Did she ever get married?"

Frye held back, not answering.

"I hear she works in a can house."

You know what he's doing, Frye thought, and he said quietly, "You're wasting your time."

Sundeen glanced at Digo, his gaze taking in the people standing off beyond Digo, and as his head turned slowly he saw the men gathered on De Spain's porch and in front of the Metropolitan, and on this side of the street the people standing watching as far down as the bank, then his gaze returned to Digo.

"If a man said that to me I'd be inclined to stomp him."

"Unless it was true," Digo said.

"Even then," Sundeen said. "Just on principle."

Frye stepped down from the doorway. He was looking at Sundeen and moved toward him quickly. Then he was standing in front of him, and looking straight ahead, over Sundeen's shoulder, he saw that Jordan had not moved.

"What if I said it to you, Phil?"

"Find out."

"I'll say something else—" Frye's hand brushed into his open coat. "You're under arrest!"

Close to him Sundeen was moving, shifting his weight, and as Frye drew his Colt he swung his left hand against Sundeen's jaw, Sundeen fell away and he was looking straight at Jordan, seeing the gun suddenly in his hand, half seeing the people scattering on De Spain's porch as he brought up his own gun, and he was conscious of himself thinking: Go down! as the rifle report filled the street. He saw the dust flick at Jordan's feet and Jordan suddenly going to the side, firing at the jail, at the doorway and then at both windows.

Get him! It was in Frye's mind as he swung the Colt after Jordan, but Digo moved. He was out of Frye's vision but less than three steps away and in the moment Digo's pistol was out and had chopped down savagely across Frye's wrist.

Stepping to the side Digo looked at Jordan eagerly. Jordan was standing still now watching the jail. "Where is he?"

"He's quit," Jordan answered.

Digo seemed disappointed, saying then, "Let's make sure." He raised his pistol and fired at the front windows, shattering the fragments of glass that remained, and when the gun was empty he called out in Spanish, "Mendez, you son of a whore, show your abusive face!"

Harold appeared in the doorway hesitantly. Seeing him Frye breathed with relief. He heard Jordan say, "Leave him alone."

"We should teach him a lesson," Digo said.

Sundeen picked up Frye's pistol. "We're going to teach both of them a lesson . . . like we did Merl White and his hardhead friends." He grinned watching Frye holding his wrist, bending it gently and opening and closing the hand.

"Digo, help the man off with his boots."

Frye turned to face Digo, who moved toward him with his pistol still in his hand. "Don't try it," he warned the Mexican.

"I've got something to convince you," Digo said. "Not without bullets—" Frye lunged toward him, but Digo was ready, side-stepping, swinging the long-barreled .44 at Frye's head, but missing as Frye feinted with his body and dodged the blow. He was crouching to go after Digo again when Sundeen's forearm closed over his throat and jerked him off balance. Digo stepped in quickly and swung his free hand into Frey's face, then waited as Sundeen threw him to the ground and straddled him, sitting on his chest.

Digo holstered his pistol. "He's something," he said, shaking his head; then pulled off both of Frye's boots and threw them toward the jail.

Harold Mendez sat down in the street and removed his boots without a word.

From the window directly above the Metropolitan Café sign, Merl White watched them get up as Digo and Phil Sundeen, mounted now, came into view reining their horses behind the two men.

"They better walk faster'n that," Merl said. The two men who had stayed with him were at the window. Haig Hanasian was in the room, but he was seated, not wanting to witness this again. Neither of the men at the window answered Merl. They watched solemnly: Digo yelling now, taking his quirt from the saddle horn and lashing it at Frye's back, forcing him to go into a run, then lashing at Harold Mendez and Harold, starting to run, hunching his shoulders ludicrously and looking back and up toward Digo as if to escape the quirt.

Merl White said, "Which one would you rather have?"

One of the men, Ford Goss, said, "I'd take Digo, with a Henry rifle."

The other man at the window did not answer. He was older than Ford by ten years and was almost completely bald. His name was Joe Tobin.

"I'd take Phil," Merl White said. "I think with an empty whisky bottle."

Ford nodded thoughtfully. "That'd be all right."

"I wouldn't cut him none, not on purpose, but I'd sure as hell bust it over his head."

Joe Tobin said now, "You notice the others aren't in it."

He was referring to the four Sun-D riders who had backed Phil Sundeen a few minutes before, but who were not in sight now.

"They're having a drink," Merl said.

"You can stand just so much," Tobin said. "I

don't know how I ever worked a day for a man like Phil Sundeen."

"It was different with Old Val," Merl told him. "Old Val worked you, but he paid pronto at the end of a drive. Sometimes even a bonus."

"Phil won't have any men left now," Tobin said. "He's gone too far."

"I think he's drunk," Merl said, squinting after the two horses nearing the end of the street now.

"He was drunk Saturday," Ford said. "He can be drunk and not show it."

"Everybody was drunk Saturday," Merl said, "but they didn't all go crazy."

"Many of them did," Haig said now, quietly.

Merl White nodded slowly. "I almost forgot about that."

"Jordan's gone too," Joe Tobin told them. "Try and figure him out."

Ford nodded. "It's got to be something against him personally, or something he's paid to do else he won't have a part of it."

"Just to have around," Tobin said, "a man like that would come high."

"He can afford it," Merl said. "Phil could pay us and still afford a dozen men like that."

"But why does he want him?"

"For days like today."

"I'll bet he pays him a hunnert a month."

Merl shrugged. "I guess a gunman comes high . . . just for the good feeling he gives you being around."

Ford was watching the street, pressing his cheek to the glass pane. "They're about out of sight."

"Will you go out and get them tonight?" Merl asked Haig.

"I was going to take you to La Noria."

"We can wait. Fact is," Merl went on, "I wouldn't mind waiting just to have a talk with this Kirby Frye. I think we got something in common."

Milmary Tindal moved out to the edge of the walk as they started down the street. She would catch glimpses of Kirby, then Phil or Digo's mount would side-step and she would not see him. When Digo's quirt went up she flinched imagining the rawhide sting and now she could not stand still. She moved along the edge of the sidewalk stretching and leaning to the side to see Kirby. Less than an hour before she had told him to get out of the store. She continued to think of that and even the quirting would not jolt it from her mind. And she was thinking that if she had been kind to him this would not be happening now. There was not time to reason it carefully; it was in her mind in a turmoil watching them move down the street. There was nothing she could do. She could make promises about the future, but right now, even though her nails dug into the palms of her hands and her knuckles showed white, there was nothing she could do.

"Do you think he'll come back?" Edith repeated.

She was in front of the Metropolitan now. Edith Hanasian stood a few feet away on the sidewalk. Milmary looked at her. "What?"

"Do you think he'll come back," Edith repeated.

Milmary was looking down the street again, but now her glance went suddenly to Edith. She had not asked herself that question and uncertainly, fearfully, she heard herself answering, "I don't know."

Edith said, "If you don't know then you haven't been treating him right."

Milmary said nothing. Edith moved to the edge of the walk and stood close to her and looking down the street they saw the horses at the far end now.

"He'll come back," she heard Edith say, and she could feel Edith looking at her closely. "Maybe it won't be for you, but he'll come back."

8

Kneeling, Frye looked through the pine branches down the slope to the dim outline of the road, then glanced at Harold Mendez hearing him moving toward him.

"What is it?"

"A wagon," Frye said. They could hear the creaking and the labored sound of a pair of horses in harness and Frye was thinking: It couldn't be them, because they wouldn't come out in a wagon. And they wouldn't come out after dark when there are other things to do.

Now they could see the shape of the wagon below them, but there was not enough moon to make out the man on the seat. He moved the team slowly, letting him have their heads going up the grade that rose gradually between the pine slopes.

Frye felt the ground in front of him until his hand found a small enough stone. He waited until the wagon was even with them, then threw the stone. It struck the wagon bed, a sharp sound in the darkness, bouncing out and almost immediately the creaking and the harness rattle stopped.

There was silence. Then from the wagon, "This is Haig Hanasian—" the words carrying clearly in the stillness.

Harold murmured, "That's his voice."

"Up here!" Frye called. He rose and stood at the edge of the jackpines waiting for Haig to reach them.

"I didn't hope to find you so quickly."

Frye took his hand as he reached them. "You came out just to find us?"

Haig nodded.

"We're obliged to you."

"How are your feet?"

"About worn through."

"I brought your boots."

"You found them?"

"They were still in front of the jail."

Frye was smiling. "We're really obliged."

"Perhaps," Haig said, "the boots will not fit now." He pulled two pairs of socks from his pocket. "These will help some. But put them on quickly, it isn't good to delay long on this road. It leads to Sun-D."

"Haig," Frye said. "We appreciate this—"

"Quickly now—"

"You go on back, Haig."

"What?"

"Danaher," Frye explained, "is due to ride by Wednesday sometime. We figured to go back in with him."

"Well," Haig said, "I can't blame you for that, but it's a long time to have to sit here."

"We'd have to hide out anyway, even in town, till we got our bearings."

Haig's dark face was serious, even saying something in a light vein. "That is done every day. This man, White, and his companions have been there since Saturday night."

"Where?"

"In my rooms."

Frye shook his head. "Right across the street."

"I was going to take them to La Noria tonight—"

"We appreciate this, Haig." Frye had spoken to Haig only a few times before this, but suddenly he felt very close to him. But he felt sorry for him at the same time and he wasn't sure why.

"Merl White is anxious to meet you."

"I guess we have something in common."

"He said the same thing." Haig lifted a .25-caliber revolver from his coat pocket and handed it to Frye. "Take this. I'd better get the wagon moving." He started to go, but stopped. "You don't have any food."

Frye shook his head. "We figured we'd grub around and make out. There's a spring back a ways." He nodded toward the deep pines.

"Tomorrow you'll have food," Haig said. "And I'll bring something for your feet." He hesitated again. "You don't have blankets."

"Or clean sheets," Harold Mendez said.

"Wait a moment," Haig told them. He hurried down the slope and returned with a rolled tarpaulin over his shoulder. "This will help some."

"Haig," Frye said, "we owe you a lot."

"You don't owe me anything. God forgive me, but I would like to see something bad happen to this Sundeen." He started to go. "You say Danaher comes Wednesday?"

Frye nodded. "That's what he said."

"To make sure, I could go to Huachuca tonight and wire him."

"He'll come," Frye said.

"I want to be there when he does," Haig said, and after that he left.

As they strung up the canvas shelter they could hear his wagon far down the grade, the faint creaking fading to silence as they gathered wood for a fire. And when the fire was burning they sat close to it, listening to the silence, then becoming aware of the night sounds, the crickets and the soft hissing of the wind through the pines.

"I'm going to quit," Harold murmured, staring into the fire. "I don't have to take this."

Frye watched the fire and said nothing.

After a moment Harold asked, "What are you going to do?"

"I'm not sure," Frye answered. "Right now, sleep."

But he did not sleep, not for some time, thinking of Danaher coming and what would happen when they rode into Randado. He knew what he would do. He was sure, even though he told Harold he wasn't sure. There was no sense in arguing with Harold. If Harold wanted to quit that was his business.

You don't have to do it though. You don't *have* to do anything. But you will, huh? You'll go through with it and have it out with Phil Sundeen and Digo . . . and Jordan, if that's the way it has to be. And Tindal and the others. Don't leave them out. "You're under arrest . . . Mr. Tindal." What do you call a man when you arrest him?

You should have stuck to mustanging.

Danaher will back you, but probably he'll give you another chance to do it by yourself if you want. He'll say, "Kirby, this is your jurisdiction. If you see fit, handle it your own way, with your own deputies. I'll only make suggestions." The Danaher let's-see-what-kind-of-a-man-you-are test. And if you're smart you'll say, "John, you can take this job and—" But something won't let you say that and you'll see it through now. Are you mad enough to see it through? Danaher said he just had to look at your beat-up face. And after what they did this morning—You're damn right I'll see it through.

Something will happen soon now to end it . . . one way or another. And that's good because it should never have started. A silly damn thing that's grown . . . no, it wasn't silly, not hanging two men, but it was stupid . . . and now there's a chance more will be dead before it's over. Sundeen will fight. Maybe he doesn't want to; maybe he knows he's gone too far, but he's not the kind who'd admit it. Like Harold said, a man who rides his horse into a saloon doesn't have to have a reason. And he didn't hire a gunman out of humility. It's too bad there isn't a way he can back down and still hold on to his self-respect. No, you have to beat him, beat him once and for all.

Tindal and the others, that's something else. They might give themselves up. If they did, Judge Finnerty would probably go light. Maybe just a fine, because he's known them all his life. They know they did wrong, else they wouldn't have run this morning. So maybe there isn't any problem . . . except living with them after. "Mr. Tindal . . . sir . . . you're under arrest." "Mr. Tindal, I wonder if I might marry your daughter . . . while you're in jail."

Wouldn't that be just fine.

You better ask Mil first.

But most of the time, until he fell asleep, he thought of Phil Sundeen, his horsebreaker and his hired gunman.

Sundeen came to Randado again late Wednesday morning. He brought with him Digo and Jordan and they went directly to De Spain's. Many of his riders had left during the past two days, including the four who had been present when he ran off Frye and Mendez, and he believed that if they were still around he would find out at De Spain's.

Sundeen stood at the bar, but Jordan and Digo took a bottle and glasses to a table.

"He drinks too much," Jordan said.

Sitting down at the table, Digo shrugged. "He holds it . . . and it's his money."

"And the more he drinks, the less you have to work."

"Watching him is work in itself."

"It's starting to wear thin."

"You get used to it," Digo told him.

"How long have you been at it?"

"Almost since the day he was born." Digo smiled. "I taught him to ride . . . how to break a horse . . . how to drink. I taught him many things."

Jordan's gaze left Sundeen standing at the bar and returned to Digo. "And now there's nothing left to teach."

Digo nodded. "Now I watch. I told this one's father I would watch him, so that's what I do."

Jordan's eyes went to Sundeen again, who stood
with his elbows on the bar and his back to them
talking to De Spain behind the bar. "Was his father
like that?"

"At times. But he worked harder than this one,"
Digo said. "I've been with him twenty years and I
know. He saw that the work was done and then he
drank. This one does what he feels like. He always
has. Even when the father was strong and would
try to break him with his fists, this one continued
his own way . . . and now it's that father who's broken. When there was no strength left to use on him,
the old man said, 'Digo, watch him—' He gave me
my name, Digo. Once it was Diego, but the old
man said it Digo and now everyone does. He said,
'Digo, watch him as I would.'" The horsebreaker
closed his eyes as if to remember the words. "He
said, 'Watch him and keep him alive as long as he's
bad, for if he dies the way he is, his next meal will
be in hell.'" Digo grinned. "That was something
for the old man to say, uh?"

"What about his mother?"

"She never counted. And now she's dead anyway."

Phil Sundeen came over to the table. He pulled
out a chair and put his foot on it and stood leaning

on his leg, looking at no one in particular. "De Spain says they haven't been in since Monday morning. And this is—"

"Wednesday," Digo said. "That's four more men you don't have."

"They might turn up. If they don't, so what? I can sign four waddies any day of the week."

"Eleven more," Jordan reminded him. "Counting the three you chased off Saturday."

"All right, eleven. I'd let go almost that many over the winter anyway. I don't need riders to scatter hay and drop salt licks. That's farmer work."

"If you don't care," Jordan said, raising his eyes to look at Sundeen, "why did we ride all the way in to look for them?"

Sundeen looked down at Digo. "He's the serious type."

"I think so," Digo answered. This was when he liked Phil the best, when he kidded with a straight face.

"The serious ones are always worried about little things," Sundeen said. "Like where to pick hands."

"I've noticed that in life," Digo said. "Some even pray before they know they're going to die."

Phil nodded. "That's the serious type."

Jordan leaned back in his chair placing his hands gently on the edge of the table. He said to Phil, "Remember what that boy said when I tried to prod him into a fight? I insulted his mother and he told me I was wasting my time."

"He was scared to fight," Sundeen said.

"Maybe so, under those conditions. But he didn't rile up and get shot. He held on until he saw an opening . . . one that you made."

Sundeen said, "What's the point?"

"The point is you tend to underestimate people. You chased that boy out of town and you don't think you'll ever see him again. Just like you think you and Digo can go on joshin' back and forth and I'll sit here and listen as long as you keep it up."

Sundeen said, "Digo . . . that's what I mean by the serious type."

Jordan rose. "I'm going to eat."

Sundeen just nodded, then followed him with his eyes as he left De Spain's.

"Don't think what you're thinking," Digo said.

Sundeen grinned. "And what's that?"

"You'd try anything once."

"How do we know he's fast? Just because some-body else said so."

"Just look at him."

"You can't go by that."

"You didn't see him draw when Harold Mendez opened up."

"Fast?"

"Fast! Listen," Digo said earnestly, "there isn't anybody in this country can touch him. I'd bet my life on it."

Sundeen shrugged. "You know how things enter our head."

"Keep that one out," Digo said, and exhaled silently as Phil straightened up, pushing the chair under the table.

"I'm going to get something to eat."

"It sounds good," Digo said.

"You get back home. Somebody's got to work."

Digo shrugged. "All right. But don't run off any sheriffs without me."

Now it was almost noon and half of the tables in the Metropolitan were occupied. Sundeen glanced at the men sitting along the counter and then his eyes went down the row of tables. There he was. Jordan. Sundeen walked toward him, but beyond he saw Tindal and Stedman sitting together and he walked past Jordan who looked up at him but said nothing.

Stedman half rose, holding his napkin to his stomach. "Phil . . . how are you?"

Tindal made himself smile, offering, "Sit down, Phil."

Sundeen pulled out one of the chairs and stepped over it sitting down.

"That's just what I meant to do." He was grinning, looking from Tindal to Stedman and said, "Haven't seen you in a few days."

"We were away," Tindal explained evasively, "on business."

"That's what I'm told."

Stedman pushed his plate forward putting his elbow on the table. "Earl Beaudry's thinking about buying some property in La Noria. Wanted us to take a look at it."

"You missed a show the other morning," Sundeen said.

Tindal nodded and now his face was serious. "You shouldn't have done that, Phil."

"You heard about it?"

"It's all over everywhere."

"Yeah, I suppose it got to La Noria else you wouldn't be back."

Stedman held his eyes on Sundeen. "Do you think we left for any other reason than because Earl asked us to come with him?"

Sundeen shook his head, grinning. "George, you old bastard, you should have been on that stage."

"Phil, I swear, when we left we didn't know Danaher was in town."

"Everybody else did."

"We can't help that."

"Why didn't Earl come back?"

"He's still looking at the property."

"Look," Tindal said, lowering his voice then, "we got no reason to lie."

Edith Hanasian came to their table and handed Sundeen a menu. His had touched her arm as he took it and she drew back.

"What's the matter, Edith?"

She returned his stare, but not his smile. "What do you want?"

Phil winked at her. "The special."

"What else?"

"Edith"—his grin widened—"you're somethin'."

"I mean to drink."

"Coffee." He was still grinning, watching her walk back to the kitchen.

"Phil, what about Kirby?" Tindal was leaning close to the table. "Is he coming back?"

"He's got no reason to."

"He won't just sit down and forget this."

"He doesn't have any choice."

"Hell he hasn't," Tindal said anxiously. "He'll go to Danaher."

"That's a long barefooted walk to Tucson."

"Phil," Stedman said as seriously as he knew how. "You got to do something."

"Like what?"

"I don't know. Explain to Danaher you were drunk and didn't mean anything by it. You're a big enough man, the most he'll do is fine you a little bit."

Sundeen looked at Stedman for a long moment. "What do you mean *you*?"

"Well, it was you that ran Kirby out."

Sundeen's face relaxed. "Why, I was working by request of the Committee. After the trouble he caused Saturday night you said we needed a new deputy and would I ask this one to leave."

Tindal's mouth opened, but no sound came from him. Stedman's words were a hoarse whisper, saying, "We never told you that!"

Sundeen shrugged. "Danaher would believe it whether it was the truth or not after the stunt you pulled Saturday."

"We can explain that to him," Stedman said hastily, "but not running off a deputy!"

"Well, now you'll have to explain both." Sundeen leaned back as Edith placed his dinner in front of him. He said pleasantly, "Where's Haig?"

"He's around."

"That's too bad, isn't it?"

She turned away without answering.

"Phil!" Tindal's tone was impatient. "You've got to think of something!"

Sundeen watched Edith until she reached the kitchen.

"That's what I'm doing."

"Be serious for a minute!"

Sundeen raised his fork and pushed it into the fried potatoes. He picked up a slice of ham with his fingers and curled it, biting off a piece. "Let me tell you something," he said, chewing the ham. "Everything I did, you did. And everything you did, I did. That includes Earl Beaudry looking over property down in La Noria. Now shut up while I eat."

They remained silent, stirring their coffee, letting it get cold and finally pushing the cups away untouched. When he was finished Sundeen stood up, taking a toothpick from the table. "Come on. I'll buy you a drink."

Stedman said absently, "I'd just as soon not."

"George, I'm not askin' you."

They went next door to De Spain's and stood at the bar, Sundeen leaning with his back against it, enjoying Tindal and Stedman's discomfort and watching Jordan, who had left the café before they did, sitting alone at a table now reading a three-day-old Tucson newspaper.

"Look at my lawyer," Sundeen said, amused. "He's not worryin' . . . and he's the serious type."

Jordan looked up, but said nothing.

Stedman finished his drink, scowling at the taste of it. "I've got to get back." He hesitated, as if expecting Sundeen to object.

"I do too," Tindal said. Stedman moved away

from the bar and Tindal followed him. "We'll see you later."

"All right." Sundeen nodded and watched them head for the door. Stedman put his hand on the knob, but stepped back clumsily against Tindal as the doors swung in abruptly.

Digo pushed past them. He was breathing heavily moving toward Sundeen and one word came from him as a gasp—

"Danaher!"

9

Frye swung down from behind Danaher and went to the jail as Danaher's posse tied up along both sides of the street. Twelve men. He recognized a few of them: three men who had been with Danaher at Galluro Station. Two others were deputies from Sonoita and Canelo. Danaher had picked them up on the way down from Tucson. All of them were heavily armed; grim-faced men who spoke little and watched Danaher for orders.

There had been fifteen originally. Three were now scouting the Sun-D buildings. To Danaher this was merely going through the motions. He knew Phil Sundeen, and he was moderately certain where to find him.

From the jail doorway Frye glanced back seeing Danaher going toward De Spain's. He's not fooling, Frye thought. And neither are the rest of them.

Dandy Jim was sitting on the floor with his back against the wall and he rose as Frye entered the office, seeing the look of surprise on Frye's face.

"I thought you'd be gone."

"If you thought that," Dandy Jim said, "why did you have that man bring food yesterday and today?"

"Well, I wasn't sure, so I mentioned it to him." He had told Haig about Dandy Jim when Haig came out to them Tuesday morning.

"He said that he saw you"—the Coyotero spoke in Spanish—"and that you would come back soon."

Frye asked, "You saw what took place the day before this?"

Dandy Jim nodded. "All of it."

"Have you seen those men today?"

"They left hurriedly before you came."

Frye's eyebrows raised. "Will you wait here?" When the Coyotero nodded he added, "Only a short time," and went out, crossing the street to De Spain's.

As he pushed through the doors, De Spain was saying, "Sundeen wanted to fight. He'd been drinking all morning and the idea of a posse on the way seemed to appeal to his sporting blood. I'd never seen a man so eager to fight . . . until Digo reminded him he didn't have enough men. Digo kept saying, 'Man, you lost eleven already—' "

Following De Spain's glance Frye saw Merl White. He was standing next to Danaher and behind him was Haig Hanasian.

"You see, besides Merl and Ford and Joe Tobin," De Spain went on, "some more left after the stunt Phil pulled with Kirby. Phil knew they had quit, but it looked as if it didn't really sink in until that moment. Still, he wasn't going to budge and he told Digo, 'Well, go on home and get who's left!' But Digo argued there was no way of telling if any of the other men were still about, and if he rode all the way to Sun-D, then came back without any-body, it would be too late to dodge Danaher's posse. Phil argued back, but you could see it sink-ing in that suddenly he was almost alone . . . that Phil Sundeen, who owned the biggest spread in San Rafael, had only Digo and a hired gunman left."

Danaher broke in, "Jordan's still with him?"

De Spain nodded. "He was when they left. You see Digo kept it up, looking like a crazy man the way he was pleading, and finally Phil said, 'All right, we'll ride out.' He looked at me then and said, 'But you tell 'em I'm coming back!' "

"I don't think he'll be that obliging," Danaher murmured. "What kind of a start did they have?"

"Not two hours," De Spain told. "But Tindal and Stedman should slow them down some."

Danaher's eyes showed surprise. "They're along?"

"They were here when Digo came in," De Spain said. "They tried to leave but Phil held them and said, by God, if he was running then they were too. They argued and pleaded until Phil pulled his gun and told them he wasn't going to hear any more."

De Spain shook his head. "They were a couple of sorry sights riding off with him."

Danaher said, "But Earl Beaudry wasn't there?"

"I haven't seen him in four days."

"They didn't say where they were going?"

"No. They couldn't go toward Sun-D because you were coming from that direction. Though it seems to me as they were going out Digo said something about circling around to Sun-D and seeing who's about, then meeting Sundeen later."

"I hope he does," Danaher said. "He'll find three men there I'm sure of. Three of mine."

Later on, while they were in the Metropolitan eating—Frye, Danaher, and the Sonoita and Canelo deputies sitting at a table together—a man came in from the street and went straight to Danaher.

"John"—he was excited and grinning, eager to see Danaher's reaction—"you sure must live right. Those three boys you mentioned watching Sun-D . . . they just brought in Digo!"

They walked across the street, pushing through the men crowding in front of the jail. Frye went in first, seeing Dandy Jim and then Digo, Digo sitting in a chair against the wall and a man standing close to him on both sides; but Danaher stopped in the doorway. He told the men outside to go over to De Spain's and take it easy.

Turning, he looked at Digo, then to the two men guarding him. "Go have a drink, boys."

They moved reluctantly and one of them said, "John, maybe you'll need a hand," glancing at Digo as he said it.

"I got two of my own," Danaher told him. "Close the door behind you." He waited until he heard it slam and then he removed his coat, not taking his eyes from Digo who sat low in the chair watching him. Danaher folded the coat deliberately and draped it over the chair by the desk.

Frye half sat on the edge of the desk with one foot on the chair. Dandy Jim stood near him. Frye moved slightly as Danaher lifted his revolver and placed it on the desk, then watched Danaher as he moved toward Digo again.

"Where'd they go, horsebreaker?"

The Mexican's chin was close to his chest, but his eyes were lifted watching Danaher and he did not answer.

Danaher stepped closer. "Where did they go?"

Digo did not move, looking up at Danaher sullenly.

"Once more. Where did they go?"

"Gimme a cigarette—"

He was saying it as Danaher hit him; his head snapped back and his eyes came full awake and he put his hand to his face.

"When I ask a question, you answer it."

"I don't know where they went."

"You were to meet them."

"No, we split up."

"You were to check for riders and then meet them."

Digo shrugged. "You know so much, why ask me?"

Danaher hit him again, his right fist landing solidly against Digo's cheek.

"The next time I'll knock you out of the chair."

Digo's hand covered the side of his face. "We did not have a place to meet."

"Maybe you've just forgotten it."

"Maybe that's it."

"Be careful, Digo."

"Listen . . . I don't know where they went!"

"You were to meet them tonight."

"There was no plan."

Danaher glanced at Frye, who had not moved from the desk and was smoking a cigarette now, and then to Dandy Jim. "We got a boy," Danaher said to Digo, "who could pick up their sign within an hour."

Digo shrugged. "All right."

"We're giving you a chance to square yourself."

"I didn't ask for favors."

"If you helped of your own accord, Judge Finnerty would go light on you."

"Go to hell."

Digo saw it coming and brought his shoulder

around, but Danaher's right hand tightened in the air and the left hand swung viciously against the exposed side of Digo's face. The chair went over and Digo sprawled on the floor.

He came to his hands and knees slowly, his eyes raised to Danaher. And as he brought his legs under him, he lunged. Danaher was waiting. He shifted his weight and his right hand swung like a mallet against Digo's head. The Mexican staggered and Danaher hit him with the other fist. Digo gasped as Danaher found his stomach. He tried to cover, but Danaher's fists broke through his guard. A jab to the head straightened Digo and a right cross slammed him against the wall.

Danaher picked up the chair, then helped Digo into it.

"I was saying, it would be easier on you if you cooperated."

Digo's mouth was bleeding and he touched his jaw, moving it gently.

"We're trying to help you."

"You know where you can put that," Digo muttered.

Danaher's arms were folded; but suddenly they uncoiled and his right fist lashed back-handed across Digo's face.

"First we want proper respect. Then the right answers."

Digo held his sleeve to his mouth, wiping it gently. "I can tell you nothing."

"Maybe," Danaher stated, "they went north."

"I don't know."

"Over toward Tubac?"

"I don't know."

"Or South. To La Noria."

"He didn't tell me."

"First to La Noria, then over the border."

"You're wasting your time."

"I've got more of it to waste than you have."

Digo's eyes stayed on the sheriff, but he said nothing.

"You know why?"

Digo shook his head. "Why?"

"Because before Christmas you'll be dead."

Digo shrugged.

"You'll hang for taking part in that lynching . . . even though it wasn't your idea."

"Maybe it was."

"Why should you protect Phil Sundeen?"

"He pays me."

"His old man pays you."

"One or the other—"

"What will you do after we hang Phil?"

"You won't hang him."

"Why not?"

"He has influence."

"All right," Danaher said, "then we'll hang you and shoot him."

"What do you mean?"

"I'll give orders to shoot him on sight. Sound asleep, taking a bath or sittin' in the outhouse, shoot him . . . and then bring him in."

Digo was silent. "But," he said finally, "you have to find him first."

"Which brings us around again," Danaher said. "Maybe you were to meet him somewhere on Sun-D land."

"He didn't say."

"In a line shack."

"He didn't say."

"Let's try the Huachucas."

Digo nodded. "All right."

Danaher's face tightened. "Watch yourself."

"You don't scare me."

Danaher stood close to him, looking down and both fists were clenched. "Digo, before the night's over I'll break you."

"I can wait."

Danaher moved a half step and his fist slammed into Digo's chest. He tried to rise, Danaher letting him, but it was momentary. Digo was pushing up, both hands on the arms of the chair, and Danaher hit him again, in the stomach and then in the face, standing in close, keeping Digo pinned against the chair, now driving both fists, grunting as he hit the Mexican, not hurrying because Digo could no longer defend himself. And when he stepped back Digo sunk into the chair, his arms hanging over the sides, and did not move.

"I've had them that tough before," Danaher said, moving to the desk. "Not many hold out."

Frye said, "He won't tell you anything if he's dead."

"If he won't alive," Danaher said, "then what difference does it make?"

"Dandy Jim asked me what you were doing. I told him and he said, 'There are many better ways to do it.'"

"I was giving him a chance, not like the Apache does it," Danaher said. "He could fight back any time he wanted."

"If he could get out of the chair."

"Don't you approve, Kirby?"

"It's none of my business."

Danaher looked at him, trying to read more than was on Frye's face, then he picked up his coat. "I'm going across the street."

"Maybe I'll work on him while you're gone," Frye said.

Danaher studied him again. "You do that, Kirby." He went to the door, but looked back before opening it. "Let me know if he tells, huh?"

When the door closed, Frye went to Digo. He pulled him forward in the chair, then stooping, let Digo fall across his shoulders. He stood up and this way carried the man up the stairs, into the cell that the two Mexicans had occupied and lowered him to the bunk. He stepped into the hall and poured water into a cup from a canvas bag that was hung there for the prisoners, then returned to Digo and raised his head gently to let the water trickle between the man's swollen lips.

Digo's eyes opened. His hand went to the cup and he emptied it drinking thirstily.

"More?"

"A little."

Frye returned with the cup filled and handed it to him. He made a cigarette while the man drank and lighted it and when Digo handed him the cup he offered the cigarette. Digo took it hesitantly, then inhaled and blew out the smoke slowly.

"When do you take your turn?" Digo asked.

"Do you think I should?"

"You have a good opportunity." Digo's eyes raised to Frye. "If it was the other way around, if I was in your shoes, I'd take a turn."

"Danaher's doing all right."

"He's doing too good."

"Just keeps it up, doesn't he?" Frye said.

"I think he must be crazy."

"That's the way he is when he makes up his mind

to something," Frye said. "He stays with it. Good for his word."

"He doesn't scare me."

"Then you're in for some more."

"That's all right."

"John gets mad and he keeps most of it inside . . . for a while. Then he has to blow off steam, like poking his fist through a door. The less you talk, the madder he gets." Frye paused. "But this time he's lucky."

"What do you mean?"

"He can blow it off on Phil."

"If he finds him," Digo said.

"There's nothing to that," Frye said. "You saw that Coyotero boy. He's the best tracker ever read sign. It would just be a matter of time." Frye grinned. "With old Danaher getting madder and madder."

"You mean that about shooting him on sight—"

"You think he was kidding? Listen, that man's word is gospel."

"I thought he was just talking."

"Danaher doesn't just talk."

Digo shook his head. "If he's so sure of getting him why does he question me?"

"It could save him a day or two if you told."

"Giving Sundeen that much more time."

"It wouldn't matter," Frye said. "Phil doesn't have a chance. And all the time the steam's building up in Danaher."

Digo was silent. He said angrily then, "This is none of his business! Why is he here?"

"Just to help out."

"Why don't you do your own work?"

"If he wants to help out it's all right with me."

Digo looked at Frye intently and asked, "Would you shoot him on sight?"

"Well, I've got no reason to."

"You'd try to arrest him for trial?"

"Probably." He knew what Digo was thinking, that if Sundeen stood trial he would most likely get off with little more than a fine. Digo had used the word influence before and there was truth to that.

"This is your territory. Would Danaher let you handle it yourself?"

"If I asked him."

"Listen." Digo was breathing heavily and his face was alive with what he was about to say. "It would be senseless for him to die just because Danaher is a madman."

"Go on."

Digo said it quickly. "If you promise to handle this yourself I'll tell where he is."

"How do you know you can trust me?"

Digo shook his head violently. "Keep Danaher off of Phil . . . swear it to God or I won't tell you!"

Frye stooped close to Digo. He said quietly in Spanish, "Where is he, man?"

"Promise in the name of God—"

Frye nodded. "I promise."

But Digo hesitated. His swollen face was strained and he closed his eyes as if in pain. "Give me another cigarette," he said, relaxing. He took it from Frye and smoked it down as he convinced himself that this was the right thing. Keep Phil alive. Perhaps it would break some of him, but it would keep him alive. He rolled toward Frye and whispered close to his ear, even though they were alone in the cell.

Danaher closed the door behind him as Frye came down the stairs.

"Where is he?"

"Upstairs."

"Did you work on him?"

Frye nodded, and he could see that Danaher was keeping himself from smiling.

"Did he tell where Phil is?"

Frye nodded again. "La Noria. You guessed it once yourself, John."

Danaher stared. There was nothing he could say.

10

"They got no business coming here," Earl Beaudry
said.

Behind him, sitting at the table, the woman
watched him as he stood in the doorway looking
past the deserted bandstand with its grayed
wooden awning to the row of two-story adobes
across the square. One of these was the La Noria
Cantina and lettered on the weathered expanse of
wall next to it was the one word, MOCTEZUMA.
Now, in the evening dusk, with rain clouds approaching, the word was obscure, losing its meaning in the fading light, though its form stood out
against the pale adobe.

The woman watched him and said nothing. This
was her adobe, hers alone since the death of her
husband three years before; though when Earl
Beaudry came she assumed a different role: the sub-
missive role she had known so well when her husband was alive. When this mood was on him it was
better not to speak at all unless he asked a direct
question.

"Why did they have to come?" Beaudry muttered.

Her eyes lifted, looking at the back of his head. No, that was not a question expecting an answer. He was talking to himself. It was bad when he was in this mood. Like Sunday night when he had beaten her for no reason at all. But he was good to her, too. He brought printed cloth . . . and flour and chocolate and— One learned to accept the good with the bad. Sometimes though, she was thinking now, it was better to speak out, then take the beating and it would be out of his system.

She was a handsome woman, firmly built, and the part of her blood that was Tarahumare showed strong in the clean dark features of her face.

"As long as they are not in this house," the woman said, "what difference does it make if they are here?"

Beaudry turned from the door, not answering her question, but came to the table and lifted the mescal bottle that was there and poured some of it into the glass he held. He had been drinking the mescal all day and it showed in his eyes and in the way he breathed with his mouth open, the corners of his mouth filmed with the colorless liquor. He returned to the doorway and looked across the square as he sipped the mescal, and now it began to rain.

"What difference does it make if they are here?" the woman said again.

"Just keep still."

"It would be less cold with the door closed," and
as she said it she wondered if this might not be going too far. But he did not turn and now she knew
that whatever it was that bothered him was a grave
matter.

She was a simple woman and she said, "Are you
thinking of your wife?"

This time he looked at her. "God, no!"

Then it was something else. Often, when he was
silent and did nothing but drink mescal, she believed he was thinking of his wife, thinking that it
was too bad she existed. Men did that, she knew.
Even unattractive men such as this one. They felt
that their wives were great weights and if they
could be free of them they would be men again.

This one came here thinking himself irresistibly
virile (until he slipped into his black mood), reliv-
ing a part of him that had been dead for a dozen
years. Even being a simple woman she could see the
kind of man that he was: at home, speaking words
to his wife only when it was necessary and sen-
tences only when they were arguing; but most of
the time silent, thinking what a great beast she was,
a dumb-eyed animal without feeling, a woman who
no longer knew what it was to be a woman, and no
longer cared. These were the men who never
looked at themselves, yet wandered from home.

Even when he came here picturing himself something else, the Mexican woman knew this about him; but she did not mind it and she thought of it little, having learned to accept the good with the bad. She did feel obligated to respect him. A man from the village had told her Señor Beaudry owned . . . how many? . . . thousands of varas of land. And he did no work! Something was said how he allowed others to use the land and they paid him for it. But, the woman would think, it is too bad he isn't attractive.

Beaudry turned now and said, speaking to himself more than to the woman, "He's over there lappin' it up, not caring a damn what happens."

"Who is?" the woman asked.

"Phil Sundeen."

"He was not here Sunday?" She could not remember the names of the two men who had come, but she knew neither had been called Sundeen.

"That was Tindal and Stedman," he said, answering the question that was in her mind.

And it occurred to her as he said their names what it was that must be bothering him. The hanging of the two La Noria men. Sunday the three of them had talked about it over and over again and in the end there had been an argument because Beaudry would not go back with them.

Tindal and Stedman. Those were the ones. Both of them beyond the middle of life, like Beaudry, though they dressed better than he did and they used language that was less coarse. She remembered now they had seemed frightened when they left. As Earl was now.

"I thought there were four of them," the woman said, remembering how they looked entering the square earlier that evening, riding almost single file.

Beaudry looked at her intently. "You've got a lot of questions."

The woman shrugged. "It doesn't matter."

"The other one works for Sundeen. That makes four."

"They are all your friends, but you don't want them here?"

"Friends," Beaudry muttered, "bringin' the law on me."

She did not understand this fully, but it seemed reasonable to say, "Then why don't you ask them to leave?"

He poured another drink before turning from her and this time didn't bother to answer.

Why don't you ask them to leave? Across the square, now, light showed in the two windows of the cantina. Why don't you ask Phil Sundeen to quit drinkin' and join the monastery? That'd make about as much sense. A woman's brain is just big enough to take her from the stove to the bed. For anything else it's got to strain. Ask them to leave . . . just like that. "Phil, you and your friends move along. This is my home . . . my second home, but I got first rights to its use." "Why sure, Earl, we'll pack up and be out by the thirty-second of December." Beaudry swore under his breath. In the doorway he could feel a mist of rain against his face as the breeze changed. All right. You can't talk nice to him. "Phil—" Look him square in the eyes and stand close and don't hardly move your mouth. "Phil, I'm not buyin' any more of that. You're not out of here in ten minutes I'll come for you with a gun!"

His elbow touched the bulk of the Colt beneath his coat as he looked across to the two lighted windows. The gun was the answer. But why take a chance facing him head on? (He allowed it to be in his mind, as if challenging Phil Sundeen was one way; although there was not even a remote possibility he would bring himself to do it.) The gun brought out the ultimate plan. The gun and the lighted windows.

Now if he were to throw some shots inside, not trying to hit anybody—If he pulled it right they'd think *posse*. Sure, the first thing they'd think of . . . a big *posse!* They'd run. By God they'd run to China!

He turned to the woman abruptly. "Didn't I bring a rifle this trip?"

You can smell a Mexican pueblo, Frye thought to himself. Even with the rain. Not a soul in the square and the adobes without windows look deserted, but you can always smell the good smell of the mesquite cook fires. If it wasn't raining there'd be people sitting by that bandstand. He was thinking then that La Noria was like a lot of pueblos; crumbling sun-dried adobe out in the middle of nowhere, but with people in it to make the cook-fire smells and keep it alive.

Frye was standing at the edge of an aspen thicket looking through the rain drizzle and across the open one hundred yards to the wide break between the adobes that showed the square. The bandstand, a dim outline of it, was on a straight line with his eyes and he knew that the cantina was along the row of adobes on the right. Merl White was next to him and Dandy Jim was one step behind.

He'll be in the cantina, Frye thought, thinking of Sundeen. Bet all you've got and borrow more to put on it, that's where he'll be. If he's not, then he's changed his ways—and you'd better change yours.

Turning his head, keeping his voice low, he said, "Merl, would you say he'd be in the cantina?"

Merl nodded and water rolled off the curled brim of his hat. "I wouldn't think about it twice," he said.

"Just go in?"

"We could wait for them to come out."

"Which could be a wet all night," Frye said.

"Let's just go in and get it over with."

"All right. You want to get the others?"

Merl said he would and moved back through the trees. Dandy Jim waited with Frye.

Now, waiting, listening to the rain, Frye thought: You shouldn't ask a question when you tell somebody what to do. He shrugged within himself. You don't have to kick Merl in the tail. No, it's not a question of the man. If you're in an order-giving position then give the damn order and don't be so damn hesitant. You don't say, "Do you want to get the others?" What if he'd said no? Watch Danaher and learn a few things. Learn how to tell men what to do.

He felt very much alone now, even though Dandy Jim was a step away from him, and he thought: I wonder if Danaher ever feels all by himself? Like the night after Galluro and John hit that man for smoking out in the open. I'll bet he felt all alone that night. It probably goes with the job. You better watch Danaher and learn how to give orders and meet the cold looks that come back half the time. But he'll be watching you tonight.

Frye had told Danaher his promise to Digo. He had promised to bring Sundeen back himself, without shooting. Danaher had agreed. This is what he had hired him for. If he didn't care to use his gun, that was all right. As long as he brought him in. Danaher mentioned that the shooting Sundeen on sight business was half scare anyway. Then Frye

172 ELMORE LEONARD

asked Danaher if he'd care to come along and Danaher said yes without hesitating.

Frye turned now, hearing the others coming up through the trees. He saw Danaher and he thought for one last time: Just tell them.

Merl White and the two other ex-Sun-D riders, Ford Goss and Joe Tobin, were following Danaher and behind them were a half dozen men Danaher had brought along to "fill out the posse."

Frye waited for all of them to come up close. "Merl and Dandy and I," he said then, "are going into the square. The rest of you will wait till we pass the first adobe, then John"—he nodded to Danaher—"you and two of your men will follow to back us up. You other four men will stay here with the horses, mounted in case anybody slips through us."

He looked at Ford Goss and Joe Tobin. "The cantina is on the right. The . . . fourth adobe down, next to a wall. You'll recognize it. Skirt around the back from here and watch the rear door."

Ford Goss said, "Do we shoot if they come out?" Almost as if he were anxious to.

"If you see them," Frye said, "you'll know. Watch Clay Jordan."

One of Danaher's men said, "I don't want any part of him."

Frye looked at Merl, then to Dandy Jim. "Ready?"

They both nodded and moved out into the open as he did. Frye and Merl carried Winchesters and Dandy Jim held a Springfield carbine up diagonally in front of him. Merl's Winchester had a large ring-type lever and he jiggled it silently as they walked across the open one hundred yards to the square.

They were almost to the first houses. Not looking right or left, Merl said, "Did you see something cross the square? The other side of the bandstand."

"I'm not sure," Frye murmured. He glanced at Dandy Jim. *"Vió algo cruzar por la plaza?"*

Dandy Jim nodded and they were sure.

Beyond the first house they stopped. They were now at the edge of the square and from here the pueblo showed more life. Not all of the doors were closed against the rain and here and there the doorways were outlined by the cook fires inside.

Merl White was looking toward the mescal shop. "The one over there with the ramada?"

Frye said, "That's right," and pointed out the adobe to Dandy Jim. It was diagonally across the square on their right; the front of it, doorway and windows, in the deep shadow of the tin-roofed ramada.

And looking at the shadowed front of the cantina Frye saw the muzzle flash as the shot was fired.

The sound of it slammed across the square and another shot followed. Three in rapid succession then, and going down it was in Frye's mind that the first one had been a rifle and the ones that followed from a .44 Colt. Merl and Dandy Jim were both on the ground with him, all of them down instinctively at the sound of the gunfire. There was a lull. Then two rifle shots, barely spaced, but there was not the lightning-quick on-off flash in the darkness this time. Coming from the side of the house, Frye thought. Suddenly there was firing from inside the cantina. Another lull followed. And again gun flashes at the front window. After that there was no more.

Rising to his feet Frye could hear the others approaching from behind, but he was still looking at the mescal shop. He saw the figure run from the darkness of the porch going directly across the square.

One! It flashed in his mind. That's all there was. He called out, "Halt!" raising his Winchester, thinking of Sundeen, and Jordan. Merl was next to him. Merl with his face against the stock and his eyes along the rifle barrel that edged steadily after the running figure.

"Halt!"

The figure broke his stride, turning, raising a rifle, and threw a shot at them. He was moving as he fired, hunched, running sideways, and his shot was high and wide. Merl hadn't lifted his head. He fired, aiming low, and the man went down, dropping his rifle, and his hands went to his thigh.

Frye was running toward him, but he stopped at the sound of gunfire coming unexpectedly from off beyond the adobes to the right. He turned, seeing Danaher running toward the mescal shop.

Then Danaher stopped and now he was looking back the way they had come, shouting something toward the openness and the dark expanse of the aspen stand beyond. As the sound of his voice echoed in the square, his riders broke from the trees, angling across the open space and were suddenly out of sight beyond the first adobe.

Merl White glanced at Frye. "Behind the cantina!"

"That's where the firing was from," Frye answered. His Winchester was trained on the wounded man who was sitting, holding his thigh and rocking back and forth as if to ease the pain; but Frye was watching Danaher. The sheriff had reached the front of the cantina. Now he disappeared into the shadows and the men who were with him followed.

Still watching, Frye moved to the wounded man. He glanced down, kicked the rifle away from him and as the man rolled back looking up, the face glistening wet and drawn with pain, he recognized Earl Beaudry.

"Don't hold the wound," Frye said. "Grab the inside of your leg and squeeze it tight." He saw Beaudry's hand groping at his knee and he said, "Up higher. It'll stop the bleeding."

Beaudry gasped, "God . . . somebody help me," then began to moan and rock back and forth again.

"Quit moving. You'll keep it bleeding."

"God, it hurts like fire!"

Frye bent closer to him. "Wait about half an hour."

"Get me a doctor—"

"You'll get one."

"Right now!" Beaudry would moan and close his eyes tightly, but open them when he spoke.

"You'll have to hold your own a while," Frye said.

"I could lose my leg!"

"Earl, what were you shooting about?"

Beaudry was silent, breathing heavily. Then he said, "I wanted to make them surrender."

Frye smiled, but to Beaudry he said, seriously, "That was good of you, Earl."

"There's Danaher again," Merl White said.

Looking up, Frye saw Danaher coming out from between the cantina and the next adobe. He had gone through, out the back door, and now had come around. Behind him were his two men, and following them were Goss and Tobin.

Approaching, Danaher called out, "Who is it?"

Frye waited until they were closer. "Beaudry."

"What was he shooting for?"

"Earl says he's on our side now."

"I guess he would," Danaher said. "Let's get him in out of the rain."

One of his men said, "He might catch cold."

Beaudry screamed as they picked him up. They started to carry him to the cantina, but he groaned, "Not there!" and pointed to the adobe across the square where the woman stood alone in the doorway. All about the square now doors were open and people were standing hesitantly watching.

The woman stepped aside to let them carry Beaudry in, then moved to the hearth and placed on more wood to build the fire, filling the kettle with water after that. Rising, she saw that they had lowered Beaudry onto the straw mattress.

Merl White asked, "What was going on back there?"

"Sundeen," Danaher answered.

"He got away then," Merl said, and seemed disappointed.

Ford Goss shook his head. "I don't want to see Jordan that close again."

"What happened?" Merl asked him.

"We were almost back of the place when the shooting started. We stopped there by a shed to see what was going to happen and a minute later the back door flies open and there's Jordan. Sundeen came next and then what must have been Tindal and Stedman. They were moving fast for the stable shed that connects to the back of the place. Then Jordan spots us and he lets go like he's six men shooting at once. His shots come zingin' through the corner of the shed keeping us back. Then they stop. I stuck my head out and like to got it blown off. Sundeen was in the saddle using his rifle while Jordan swung up. See, they must of had them already saddled. Then when we heard the horses Joe and me ran out, but all four of them were around the stable shed before we'd fired twice."

Frye said, "John, I saw your boys come out of the trees."

Danaher shook his head. "They won't get them. It's too dark out in the brush. Sundeen could hold up and let them ride right by."

"And with the rain," Frye added, "by morning all the tracks'll be gone."

Danaher took a cigar from his pocket, bit the tip off and lit it. "We've got time."

"They're probably in Mexico by now," Merl White said.

"Well," Danaher said, "that's all right too. If they stay hidden, the world's a better place to live in. If they come back, we take them." Danaher looked at Frye. "What do you want to do?"

"Take Earl back."

Merl said, "Maybe some of us could stay here-abouts and look around."

Frye nodded. "If you want to that'd be fine."

"You never know," Merl said.

11

They had stretched a tarp over the borrowed wagon that carried Earl Beaudry and most of the way back to Randado Frye sat with him in the close darkness of it. The rain stopped during the early morning and they rolled back the tarp; but it was daylight before they reached Randado. There were figures in doorways and people standing by ramada posts watching solemnly as they passed down the street; watching curiously as they stopped in front of the doctor's adobe and lifted out Beaudry, straw mattress and all.

They had all returned except Merl White, Goss, Tobin and Dandy Jim.

Danaher's men moved off across the street to the boardinghouse, but the sheriff and Frye waited to hear the doctor's report.

And after that, out in the street again—

"He's got nothing to worry about," Danaher said. "When the bullet doesn't go all the way through, then it's time to worry."

Frye's hand moved over his jaw, feeling the beard stubble there. "I better go tell Mrs. Beaudry."

"What about the other women?"

"I'll have to tell them too."

"Why don't you go over and talk to the Tindals? I'll go up and see Beaudry and Stedman's women."

"I could talk to them, John."

"Seeing the Tindals is enough," Danaher answered.

"Now?"

"Might as well. I'll see you back at the office."

Frye watched Danaher cross the street diagonally toward the last adobe building. The small residential hill was just beyond. Then he turned and crossed the street himself in the direction of Tindal's store.

Milmary opened the door for him. She had been standing by it, watching, waiting for him to come, going over in her mind the words she would use, but now he was here and she said nothing.

Frye removed his hat feeling it sticking to his forehead and nodded solemnly. Milmary passed him and his eyes followed her to the counter. Her mother stood behind it.

"Mrs. Tindal. Your husband's all right."

Her mouth formed a smile, but the rest of her face did not smile, and her eyes were picturing something that was not in the room. He could see that she was trying to be calm, and pleasant. And it went through his mind: Why did she ever marry him? She was a plain woman, her hair parted in the middle and drawn back tightly into a bun, though there were thin wisps of hair not in place. He felt sorry for her because he could picture her combing her hair, trying to make it look attractive; but it was not attractive now, and probably it never had been. He felt sorry for her because she was plain, because no one would attach any importance to her, not even in little things, though perhaps Mil would. He could picture Tindal scarcely paying any attention to her when she spoke. But she would serve him and smile when he expected her to smile and praise him when he expected to be praised. And Frye felt sorry for her because he knew she needed to be held; but there was no one, not even Tindal if he were here.

"Mrs. Tindal, I'm awful sorry about this—"

He hesitated. She was looking at him, but not trying to answer. "I wanted to talk to you before, but I never got the chance."

Milmary asked, "Where is he?" Her voice seemed natural.

He looked at her, conscious of his beard and his hair stuck to his head from the hat being on so long and his damp clothes shapeless and dirty looking. Maybe he smelled. All that riding, then under that hot tarp with Beaudry. He could feel her eyes on him when he was not looking at her.

He told them everything then, beginning with their arrival at La Noria. He told it quietly and most of the time he looked at Mrs. Tindal.

"Sundeen forced your husband to go with him, Mrs. Tindal. We know that for a fact."

Milmary said, "Be sure you're not blamed for anything."

"De Spain will testify that Sundeen forced them to leave his place at gun point."

"That's noble of Mr. De Spain."

"Mil, why don't you talk like you've got some sense?"

She held his gaze silently for a moment. "Are you finished now?"

"I guess I am." He started to put on his hat.

"Kirby."

He looked at Mrs. Tindal. She had not spoken before and now the sound of her voice surprised him.

"Did you see him, Kirby?"

"No ma'am, I didn't."

"What will happen to him?"

"Nothing, Mrs. Tindal. This is kind of a game with Phil Sundeen. Soon he'll get tired of it and come home."

"He won't do anything to them?"

"No ma'am, I'm sure he won't."

Milmary said, "But when he comes back—"

Frye nodded once. "He'll stand trial."

"Will you take him to Yuma, too?"

He ignored Milmary's question. "Mrs. Tindal, you can figure your husband won't get more than a fine, if that. Judge Finnerty's a friend of Mr. Tindal's." Frye smiled. "You know he wouldn't send him to Yuma."

Milmary asked abruptly, "But what happened to Mr. Beaudry?"

"He was shot in the leg trying to run."

"How do you go about dodging that blame?"

"Mil, he fired on us first."

"Did you shoot him, Kirby?"

"No."

"That was decent of you, since he helped get you your job."

He looked at Mrs. Tindal instead of answering. "Can I do anything for you, ma'am?"

"Haven't you done enough?" Milmary asked.

He thought: You asked for it. But she could have thought of something better than that to say. He felt his temper rise, hearing her words again in his mind. He moved to the door putting on his hat, then touched the brim to them and stepped outside.

Maybe this is a good thing, he thought as he walked toward De Spain's. You get to know a person better when something like this comes up. After you're married, how'd you like to have that the rest of your life, everytime you have a disagreement? She'd give you that silent act. If you said something she had to answer, then she'd come back with the ice-water tone. I think I'd rather have a woman who throws plates. She'd get it out of her system and it would be over with. Well, enough's enough. If she wants me, she knows where to come.

He told these things to himself but he did not completely believe them. They made him feel better, that was all.

He nodded to a group of men standing in front of De Spain's, then started across the street toward the jail. His back was to them when he heard one of them say, "Some people think they're pretty goddamn big."

Frye stopped and half turned. One of the men was holding on to a support post staring at him defiantly. He was drunk and without the post would have fallen into the street. Behind him, four men stood close as if in conversation. They paid no attention to the drunk, though before, when Frye nodded, the five of them had been standing together.

He continued across the street and entered the jail office. Harold Mendez came away from the window as he closed the door.

"Harold." He nodded to the jailer. "I see you fixed the windows."

"Digo did," Harold said, "he broke them. I tied his feet and held a shotgun behind his back while he did it."

Frye took off his hat and slumped wearily into the chair in front of the desk. He leaned forward to unfasten his spurs, then going back, lifted his feet to the desk and crossed them.

"I saw you come in with Beaudry," Harold said. "One of Danaher's men left his gear here. When he came in for it, he told me the whole thing."

Frye was silent. Then he said, "How are they talking about it at De Spain's?"

"I haven't been over there."

"Did you see that just before I came in?"

Harold nodded. "What did he say?"

"Some people think they're pretty goddamn big."

"He was drunk," Harold said. "When he's not cleaning the livery he's drunk. You never know what he'll say."

"He didn't say it. The four behind him did. They poured the words in and he used them."

"You have to expect a certain amount of that."

"What are they saying, Harold?"

"Well . . . last night a few men came over from De Spain's and one of them asked if the rest of the people could consider themselves safe or should they run too. It was supposed to be cutting, but he sounded as if he was reading it. He said when the manager of the bank and the town's leading merchant have to leave town, then it's time to look more closely at the one who's chasing them, and reconsider. Something like that."

"Did you mention," Frye said, "Sundeen's Colt making them run?"

"They're going back before that," Harold said. "Many of them took part in the hanging even if they didn't tie the knots. They're not wanted, but they probably still feel obliged to share a little of the blame with Tindal and Stedman. The way to do that is oppose you."

"How do they feel about Sundeen?"

"He's the biggest man around here. They're awed by him, even if they don't like him, and they don't see how a young deputy who's only been here a month gets off chasing him out of town. People are scared to death of Phil Sundeen, but they still look up to him. Because he's got money if for no other reason. A man with money must be important."

"Which is how the whole thing started," Frye said.

"That's right."

Frye shook his head. "There must be some sensible people here."

"Plenty," Harold answered. "They're the ones that hardly even talk about it. They probably think we're all children."

Frye was silent, but after a moment he said, "Harold, I'm tired."

The jailer nodded. "I know what you mean."

When Danaher came in Frye was shaving in front of a mirror propped on the desk. He was sitting on the edge of the chair and turned to look at Danaher as he entered.

"How was yours?" Danaher asked.

"Well, I didn't get the red carpet."

"Maybe you should have done that first." Danaher nodded to the razor.

"I needed more than a clean face."

"Ten years from now you and Mil will think back on this and you might even smile."

"How did you do?"

"The ladies were obliged to greet me with cold stony eyes and expressions that would've cracked like china had you touched them."

"How'd you expect them to treat you?"

"Kirby, I never *expect* anything."

"Yes sir," Frye said, not knowing, or caring, how Danaher would take it.

"You need sleep," Danaher said.

He wanted to say it again, because he was suddenly near the end of his patience. Yes sir—something a kid would say in a tone all of its own, thinking he was smart. He realized this, and held on; and moving the razor down his jaw line slowly, he said, "John you want to get something to eat first?"

They went to the Metropolitan and throughout the meal they spoke little. Once, Danaher said, "You feel all alone now, don't you?" and this stayed on Frye's mind even after they left the café. Maybe Danaher could read his thoughts—like when he was hiring him for the job after the Galluro thing. At the boardinghouse they bathed and went to bed, but before falling asleep Frye thought: He was talking from experience. Danaher feels alone too. And that was some consolation. Enough to let him fall asleep almost right away.

In the evening they ate at the Metropolitan again. Haig Hanasian served them and at the end of the meal he leaned close to Frye and said, "If you go out again, I would look upon it as a privilege to be along."

"We're not sure we will."

"Just if you do."

They returned to the jail office to smoke and theorize now. They would wait for Sundeen's move, but they could be thinking while they waited. Harold brought a bottle and glasses and in the semi-darkness they sipped whisky and talked until late.

Probably Sundeen had taken them across the border. That was logical; that made more sense than anything else. Still, Sundeen was not a man who lived by his reason. Frye remembered Danaher's words earlier in the day, "I never *expect* anything." That was the way to consider Sundeen. Don't say, "He probably did this." You'll find out he did the opposite.

So they didn't take for granted that Sundeen crossed the border. And the more they thought about it, the stronger the possibility was that he had not.

"He could even swing back this way," Danaher said, "to see what happened to Digo. He could even have in mind raising a fighting force. He's bullheaded enough."

"What about Tindal and Stedman talking him into giving up?" Frye suggested.

"Not a chance."

"They could circle up to Tucson and turn themselves over to Judge Finnerty."

"I don't think so."

"Digo talked him into running when he was set against it."

Danaher nodded thoughtfully. "That's right."

"Maybe he's not the stone wall we give him credit for," Frye said.

"But you can't predict the bastard. That's the trouble."

They were in the office again the next morning, Danaher having decided to return to Tucson since there was nothing to do but wait, and he was getting ready to go when Ford Goss rode in. Ford looked drained; as if he'd been riding all night.

He swung off, seeing them standing in the doorway, and the first thing he said was, "Dandy caught their sign!"

12

They rode southeast from Randado, Ford Goss showing the way, his saddle on a fresh mount and Ford in it again after a rest that lasted only as long as it took to drink a cup of coffee and eat a plate of meat and beans. He was bone tired, but he stayed in the saddle and followed his own trail without any trouble, without even thinking about it, because this was not something new. He couldn't count the number of watches he'd stood over a night herd, then stayed in the saddle the whole next day until sundown. It was part of a riding job.

At their first rest, Ford related the details of finding Sundeen's trail. How they had ridden south from La Noria and swung east along the border for half a day without seeing a track of any kind. Merl said maybe they crossed during the rain; but maybe they didn't go over the border after all, and that was worth checking. So they started bearing north in a wide circle. West was open country, but northeast from La Noria were the Huachucas and that way made more sense. By midafternoon they had

picked up four tracks bearing more to the east,
Dandy Jim spotting the hoof marks no white man
could have. They followed. At a waterhole farther
on they found two cigarette stubs and there the
tracks of four horses were unmistakable. Then luck
hit them right in the face. "Good luck that only
comes from living right," Ford said. An hour from
the waterhole they came across two Tonto-Mojave
women dressing down a buck. The women told
Dandy Jim they had watched from a distance as a
party of white men shot the buck and took its
hindquarters. Now they were only taking what had
been left. Dandy asked them what the men looked
like. They described each man—and then there was
no longer any doubt. That evening when they
camped, they matched to see who was going to ride
all night to Randado. Ford lost.

Danaher was along with his six men—Danaher
riding easily for a big man, unconcernedly, a cigar
clamped in the corner of his mouth.

Frye and Haig Hanasian rode side by side most
of the time. Frye slouched in the saddle, his
straight hatbrim low over his eyes. He could have
been asleep, the loose way he followed the dun
gelding's motion; but he was not asleep and he
missed nothing.

Haig Hanasian rode in silence. He made no com-
ment about the weather, nor about the trail becoming rougher as they climbed into the foothills of the

Huachuca range. Haig's hat was narrow-brimmed and he wore a full suit and a cravat. Everything about him seemed out of place except the expression on his face. Frye noticed this. Haig's silence and his masked expression told nothing; yet by their presence they told everything. At least to Frye. He remembered Edith mistaking him for Sundeen the night he entered the café late, as if she had been expecting Phil. Probably something was going on between them, Frye thought. Haig found out. And now he wants to do something about it.

Before noon they reached the camp where Ford had left Merl. Riding at night it had taken Ford seven hours to reach Randado; returning during daylight they did it in almost half that time.

"Merl and Joe and Dandy stayed the night here," Ford explained.

"You must have been close to them," Frye said. It was a dry camp and there had been no fire.

"So close we had to stop when we did," Ford said, "for fear of riding on them in the dusk. Merl said him and the boys would go on at daylight, but that we'd be able to follow him easy."

They rested the horses, then moved on following Merl's sign, crossing a three-mile length of meadow where the wild grass was broken and bent forward in a narrow path down the middle. Through scattered pine stands they followed branches Merl had broken and left hanging. Over rocky ground there were stones set in a row pointing the way. They could have followed the horse tracks, but this saved time and time was the important element. They entered a draw that was narrow and overgrown with brush and they moved through it single file, feeling the gradual rise and when it opened they were high up on a bench that looked down on a valley and the tops of jackpines far below. Dandy Jim was there waiting for them.

He led them along the bench, then down a slope through dim, silent timber. At the bottom, watering their horses in a stream, Merl White and Joe Tobin were waiting.

Merl was squatting on his heels at the edge of the stream. He looked over his shoulder, then rose as Dandy Jim brought them in.

"Where you been?"

Danaher stepped out of the saddle. "The other side of the mountain pickin' our noses."

Frye's gaze moved over the small clearing. He saw traces of the fire that had been smothered out, and close to him, at the edge of the clearing, the grass was trampled and broken off where the horses had been picketed. He watched Dandy Jim cross to the stream removing his red cotton headband. He dipped it in and out of the water quickly, then spread it out and rubbed mud into it from the damp bank. He shook it, then spread it out again to let the sun dry the mud. They're close, Frye thought.

He heard Merl White saying, "We got us a problem. They split up here."

"What?" Danaher was lighting a cigar but he held it and the match went out in his hand.

Frye swung down and let his horse go to the stream. "Maybe they split up leaving here," Frye said, "but met again further on."

Merl shook his head. "Three of them went due north up the stream, but one crossed over and followed it down the other way."

Danaher lit his cigar and blew on it slowly. "Now which one would that be?"

"You wouldn't think Tindal or Stedman," Frye said.

"Unless," Danaher said, "one of them got a chance to sneak off during the night."

Frye asked Merl, "Where'd he cross?"

"Right there where your horse's watering."

"They were grazed over on the other side," Frye said. "That means he'd have to have brought his horse right through camp to cross the stream there."

"I didn't finish," Merl said. "We figure whoever it was, left a few minutes before the others, and in daylight. Dandy crossed over and followed his sign a ways, down the stream about a hundred yards, then up into the trees. Dandy says up there in a clearing the man had stopped. You can see this camp from there. The man waited there a while, least long enough to smoke a cigarette, because the stub of it was there. And he must have been watching the others."

"The careful type," Danaher said.

Frye said, "And he smokes cigarettes. You ever see Tindal or Stedman with anything but a cigar?"

"No," Danaher answered, "I don't believe I have."

"Are you thinking," Frye asked, "what I'm thinking?"

"Probably so," Danaher said. "Sundeen wouldn't be likely to walk out on his old committee friends after going to so much trouble to bring them along. And he doesn't strike you as the kind who'd sit over there and smoke a cigarette once he'd made up his mind to move. That leaves one man. Jordan. If they had an argument and Jordan walked out, I think he'd be inclined to watch them till they were out of sight."

Frye looked at Merl. "How far did Dandy follow him?"

"About an hour."

Frye went over to Dandy Jim and the Coyotero, squatting down, looked up at him and grinned as if to say: I've been waiting for you.

Danaher watched them and it reminded him of

Galluro to see the two squatting together drawing lines on the smoothed dirt. He drank a cup of cold coffee from Merl's canteen, then saw them stand up.

The Coyotero took the cloth that was spread open next to him, folded it into a triangle and tied it over his long hair, knotting it in back. He looked like a color picture Danaher had once seen of a pirate, only now the headband wasn't red; it was a dull brown color that wouldn't be seen through the trees or stand out against rock. Then Frye came toward him.

"John, Dandy and I figure we can take Jordan before he gets anywhere near the border."

"Is that so?"

"Assuming he'll follow the stream as long as it bears generally south, we can make a straight line and be waiting for him when he comes out of the valley."

"Dandy knows the country?"

"Like his hand."

"Just the two of you?"

"We'd go a lot faster."

Danaher shrugged. "You're in charge."

"You'll keep after the others?"

"Of course."

"We'll catch up with you later."

"Kirby, just keep one thing in mind. He gets paid for carrying a gun."

Dandy Jim leading, they splashed over the shallow stream, then followed Jordan's tracks along the bank and up to the clearing where he had waited. From there Jordan had gone down again, following the stream south. But now Frye and the Coyotero slanted up through the timber, their horses going slower, more carefully, as the slope became steeper, then making switchbacks through the trees as the pines near the rim grew more dense. At the top they looked back. They could see the stream and the camp they had left far below on the other side, but there was no movement and they knew Danaher had gone on.

Daylight was beginning to fade, but here was open country dipping and rolling in long gradual swells and they gave the horses their heads, letting them run hard in the cool breeze of evening. Then, in gray dimness, they rode down the long sweep of land that stretched curving downward to the mouth of the valley.

Now, looking back into the valley they could see gigantic rock formations tumbled through the wild brush of the valley floor. Following the stream, Jordan would move slowly. And the rocks would slow him even more, Frye thought. He was confident that Jordan had not left the valley before they arrived to seal its exit.

Frye asked, "Where does the stream end?"

The Coyotero pointed to the trees, now a solid

black mass between the steep sides of the valley.
"Beyond there the time it would take to ride one
hour."

Then that's where he will camp, Frye thought. By
water. Because he doesn't know when he will see it
again. And he would camp early; rest the horse
well; and make the border in one ride.

"It is too wide here to wait for him," Frye said.

Dandy Jim nodded, agreeing. They moved their
horses into the mouth of the valley that began to
narrow abruptly after only a few hundred yards
and now they angled toward the near side and left
their horses in the dense pines that grew along the
slope. They moved farther in on foot, then climbed
up into the rocks to wait.

"It will be all right to smoke," Dandy Jim said,
which was his way of asking for a cigarette. Frye
made them and they smoked in silence. Afterwards,
they ate meat which they had brought and drank
water from their canteens. They smoked another
cigarette before going to sleep.

At first light, the Coyotero touched Frye on the
shoulder. He came awake, sitting up, looking out
over the rocks to the floor of the valley.

"This is a good place," the Coyotero said.

"Even better than it looked in the dark," Frye
agreed. Across to the other slope was less than three
hundred yards; then, to the right, another three
hundred to the trees and tumbled rocks through

which Jordan would come. The trees seemed less dense on this side of the valley, which meant Jordan would likely be bearing to the near side. That, Frye thought, would make it all the better.

They decided how they would do it, watching the trees as they talked.

After, Frye rolled four cigarettes and gave them to Dandy Jim with matches, then watched as the Coyotero scrambled down the rocks. First he would check the horses, then return to the pines directly below Frye ready to run out and disarm Jordan after Frye commanded him to halt. Dandy Jim had said, "Why not shoot him from here?" But Frye explained that it would be better to take him back as a prisoner.

And now he waited, leaning on his left side, looking through a groove in the rocks in front of him. His Winchester rested in this V and from time to time he would sight on the break in the trees through which he expected Jordan to come.

The rocks that jutted out from the opposite slope were clean and clear in the early morning sunlight, but the floor of the valley, almost all the way across, was still in shadow. He could hear the cries of birds back in the trees in the direction he watched, and the soft sound of the breeze in the pines. The rocks beneath him were cold and he thought, feeling the dampness of the rocks but meaning the entire cool early morning stillness of the valley: By the time the sun is high enough to warm it, this will be over.

Keep listening to the birds. They'll give you warning when he comes. If they are in the lower trees they'll fly up as he passes them.

He looked at the shadow below him and he thought: Like rolling up a black rug. You almost see it getting shorter. Eight o'clock? Something like that. He's not rushing into anything. He looks ahead, and this morning he's making sure his horse will take him to the border. It would've been good to have seen what happened between him and Sundeen. Maybe it was payday and Sundeen didn't have the money. Maybe it was as simple as that.

He could not hear Dandy Jim below him and he did not expect to. This is his meat. He's Apache and could sit in an ambush for ten years if he thought it was worth waiting for.

He could not hear the horses either. Purposely they were both geldings. There would be nothing between them that would be worth nickering about.

He saw the birds rise from the trees. They were in a flock, now swooping and rising as one, and they flew out of sight up the valley. Frye rubbed out his cigarette.

Jordan stopped at the edge of the trees. He dismounted and adjusted his cinch, pulling it tighter. Then he mounted and rode warily out of the trees.

Frye's front sight covered Jordan's left side, the sight barely moving, barely lowering as Jordan came on. The Winchester was cocked.

Mr. Jordan, Frye thought looking down the barrel, you're about to make a decision. And you won't have time to change your mind once you make it. The front sight dropped an inch as Jordan drew nearer to the slope and Frye's finger was light against the tightness of the trigger. Just flick it, he thought, and you've solved everything. No, let's take him home.

Now Jordan was even with him and Frye knew that this was as close as he would come.

"JORDAN! THROW UP YOUR HANDS!"

The words echoed in the narrowness and Jordan made his decision. Frye saw the horse wheel suddenly toward the slope and rear up, rearing the same moment he fired.

Jordan was reining again, pulling the horse's head to face the trees, and the horse moved with a lunge that took it almost to a dead run the first few yards. Frye hurried the next shot and it was low and suddenly he had to go down as Jordan returned the fire, emptying his gun, at fifty yards, straight up through the V where Frye was crouched.

Five shots! Frye was up, seeing Jordan slapping the gun barrel across the horse's rump. He heard firing below him. Dandy Jim. Jordan was running now, not looking back, his right leg out of the stirrup, holding close to the horse's off side. Frye fired, aiming at the horse now, but the horse did not go down. And in a moment it was too late. Jordan had disappeared into the trees.

13

How could you miss! Frye thought. He was angry because he had hurried the shot. Missing Jordan the first time was not his fault: the horse had reared. But the second shot: Jordan was running, for seconds less than a hundred yards away, and he had let himself be hurried. Now, there was not time to stand thinking about what he should have done, though as he went down the slope, scrambling from rock to rock, making sure of his footing, then sliding down on the loose gravel, he could still see Jordan crouched low in the saddle laying his pistol barrel across the horse's rump.

And as Frye reached the base of the slope, it went through his mind: Maybe you did hit him, but not where it would knock him down.

Dandy Jim approached along the edge of the pines. He was on his gelding and leading Frye's.

"How could we have missed?"

The Coyotero shook his head. "But I think we took the horse."

Frye looked across the open three hundred yards

to the denseness of the trees and the rocks beyond.
"He could be waiting for us to come after him," he
said, squinting toward the trees, dark and unmov-
ing beyond the sunlight. "But probably he won't
wait, because he doesn't know how many we are."
He looked at Dandy Jim, but the Coyotero's face
was without expression and he did not speak. "If
his horse was hit, it might have dropped just in the
trees. Then he would have gone on afoot . . . or
waited, thinking one place to stand was as good as
another."

Now the Coyotero nodded.

Frye swung up. "We could talk about it a long
time, but there's only one way to find out for sure."
He was looking at Dandy Jim as he kicked his dun
forward and he saw a smile touch the corner of the
Coyotero's mouth.

Riding across the meadow Frye could feel his
shoulders pulled up tensed and he told himself to
relax, thinking: A shoulder's no good against a .45
slug, is it? Still, he could feel the tightness inside of
him and just telling himself to relax wasn't enough.

They covered most of the distance at a trot, then
slowed to a walk the last few dozen yards and entered the trees this way, their carbines ready. There
was no sound and slowly Frye could feel the tightness within him easing. If he's close, he thought, he
would have fired when we were in the open or just
coming in.

The Coyotero pointed ahead and Frye could see clearly the path Jordan's horse had made breaking into the brush. His gaze lowered, coming back along the ground, and now he noticed the streaks of blood that were almost continuous leading from where they stood to the brush clumps.

"There's no doubt we got his horse," he said to Dandy Jim.

The Apache nodded, answering, "It won't last very long."

"We'd better go on foot."

"I think so," the Apache said. "Listen," he added then. "I think I should go first, and you should follow, leading the horses."

"Why should you go first?" Frye said.

"Because I always do."

"There's nothing that says you have to." He could see that the Coyotero wanted to do this to protect him. "I'm the one responsible for bringing him back," Frye said.

"I think we're wasting time now," Dandy Jim said. He turned abruptly and started for the brush leaving Frye with the horses. But as he passed between the first clumps he looked back and saw that Frye was following him, leading the horses, holding the reins in his left hand. He had replaced the Winchester in its saddle boot and now he had drawn the Colt and was carrying it in his right hand.

They moved steadily through the brush patch

stopping when they came to the end of it. From here the signs of blood angled more to the left, gradually climbing a bare slope, a slide of loose shale that reached openly almost to the rim high above them. He could be waiting up there, Frye thought. But if he didn't wait before, why should he now?

Halfway up the slope the blood tracks veered abruptly and slanted down again into the trees. His horse couldn't make it, Frye thought. They followed, the shale crunching, sliding beneath their feet as they went down, and in the trees again it was quiet.

Now Frye watched Dandy Jim who was almost twenty yards ahead of him. He would see the branches move as the Coyotero moved steadily along, but he would hear no sound. Farther along, he began to catch glimpses of the stream through the pine branches to the right. Then ahead he could see a part of the stream in full view, and as he looked at it he saw Dandy Jim stop.

The Coyotero went down on his stomach, remaining there for what must have been ten minutes before rising slowly and coming back, running crouched, toward him.

"His horse," Dandy Jim said, reading him.

"Where?"

"By the stream."

"And you didn't see the man?"

"No. The horse is at the edge of the stream, part of it in the water."

"Dead?"

"Not yet."

"Quickly then."

The Coyotero turned and crept back toward the stream. Frye followed, but left the horses where they were.

Jordan's horse was at the edge of the stream, its hind quarters in the water and its head up on the bank. As the swell of stomach moved, blood poured from a bullet wound in the horse's right flank. It colored the water, red as it came from the horse, brown fading to nothing as it poured into the water and was moved along by the small current.

The horse had been shot again just behind the right shoulder; and as Frye started to cross the stream, looking down at the horse as he stepped into the water, he saw where another bullet had entered the withers; probably his first shot and he wondered briefly why it had not killed the horse on the spot.

He saw Jordan's footprints before he stepped out of the water. They bore to the left following the stream.

He signaled to Dandy Jim, who ran back through the trees for their horses. Then, watching him as he brought them back, he saw the Coyotero go to one knee next to Jordan's horse, then saw him bring out his knife and cut the animal's throat in one slash. The Coyotero brought their horses across then.

"Listen," Frye said, "let's do it this way now. You go up the slope and work along the edge. I'll stay on his sign and from time to time watch for you to signal. He won't climb out of here now, not without a horse."

"But he could when night comes," Dandy Jim said.

"We've got to pin him down before that."

They arranged a signal: every ten minutes the Coyotero would imitate the call of a verdin. If he located Jordan he would imitate a crow. Then he would either return to Frye or lead him on to Jordan by the same signals.

Frye watched Dandy Jim ride out of sight into the pines before he went on, following Jordan's footprints: at first, the marks of high-heeled boots that were easily read in the sand; but farther on, as the sand gave way to rocky ground, the marks were less apparent. And often he went on without a sign to follow, choosing one path through the rocks rather than another because it seemed more direct, less likely to bring him back to a point he had already passed.

Twice he heard the verdin, perhaps a hundred yards ahead of him and up on the slope.

Then again. This time it seemed to be closer.

Frye entered the narrowness of a defile and stopped in the deep shadow of it to drink from his canteen. He took a bandanna from his pocket and wetting it, wiped his horse's muzzle, cleaning the nostrils. Then, as he started out again, he stopped and drew back into the shadows instinctively as the sound of gunfire came from somewhere off to the right up on the slope.

Two shots from a revolver and a heavier report that was still echoing through the rocks.

Springfield, Frye thought. Dandy's on him and it must have been unexpected with no time for the signal. He reached past the horse's shoulder and drew his Winchester and turning back, his eyes momentarily caught a movement in the lower pines. He raised the Winchester, waiting as the minutes passed.

There!

The figure darted from the trees running crouched low. The sound of the Springfield came from higher up on the slope and the split-second he heard it Frye fired.

Too late. He was behind rocks now.

Frye had waited because he had not been able to identify the figure, and by the time the Springfield told him who it was, it was too late.

But now you're sure, Frye thought, looking at

the rocks where Jordan had disappeared. Now you
know where he is . . . and all you have to do is go in
and get him. Or wait him out.

He studied the terrain thoughtfully. He was
slightly higher than Jordan's position and beyond
those rocks there appeared to be an open meadow.
Probably, Frye thought, that's why he turned into
the pines. He didn't want to cross the open. Not
now. To the east was the pine-thick slope, and
Dandy Jim. Frye was to the south. Beyond the
stream was the steep slope to the west. It could be
climbed, but much of it was bare rock and it would
take time . . . if Jordan ever reached it, which was
improbable. Still, Jordan could move around to
some degree in a fifty-yard radius of rock and
brush.

All of this went through Frye's mind and he concluded: He has to be pinned to one spot before dark
and not be able to leave it.

He was sure that the Coyotero realized this.
Now it was a question of working together. But
first, Frye thought, tell Dandy where you are.

He aimed quickly at the spot where Jordan had
disappeared and fired. Now be ready, he thought.

The Springfield opened up. One . . . two . . . on
the second shot Frye was moving, running veering
to the left . . . three . . . diving behind a rock covering as a revolver shot whined over his head and ric-

ocheted off the crest of the rock. Frye exhaled, close to the ground. Now they both know.

He crawled along behind the cover of the rocks, then raised his head slowly until he was looking at Jordan's position from another angle. But he could not see the gunman even from here.

A little more around, Frye thought. And a little closer. He brought the Winchester up and fired quickly.

The Springfield answered covering him. Frye was up running straight ahead, then to the left again. He found cover, went to his knees, but only momentarily. The Winchester came up with his head—

Jordan! A glimpse of him disappearing, dropping into a pocket among the rocks.

Frye fired, levered and fired again—four times, bracketing the pocket and nicking one off the top of the rocks where Jordan had gone down.

It had worked. Jordan was still behind cover, but now he could not move, not three feet without exposing himself; and even darkness would do him little good.

Now we'll see how good he is, Frye thought. We'll see how good his nerves are—and if he has any patience. I should have told Dandy how he is with a gun. No, he already knows it. He was inside the jail when Jordan let go at Harold Mendez. And he heard how Jordan came out of the La Noria mescal shop. So he won't underestimate him.

Frye was on his stomach, but with his elbows raising him enough to see over the rocks and down the barrel of the Winchester in front of him. Mesquite bunched thickly all around him and even with his eyes above the rocks he knew Jordan would not see him. Not unless he fired. And Frye had no intention of firing. Jordan was flanked. He was cut off from water and cut off from escape—unless pure luck sided with him.

For the second time this day Frye settled down to wait. He knew Dandy Jim would do the same. He was Apache and would not rush into something that could be solved with patience. Dandy Jim has it figured out better than you, Frye thought. He's done this more times than you have. Let the quietness work on Jordan. Let him realize he's alone and there's nothing he can do about it. Let him think until he's tired of thinking. Then he will do something. He might even give himself up. If he does, wrap fifty feet of rope around him and still don't trust him. But it won't be that way, will it?

Frye waited and the time passed slowly.

It was less than two hours later, though it seemed longer, when Jordan started to do something.

"Frye!"

Frye looked up at the unexpected sound of his name. He could not see Jordan, but he knew it was

Jordan who had called. He watched, feeling the stock of the carbine against his cheek, and did not answer.

"Frye!"

He waited.

"Goddamn-it that's your name, isn't it!"

I didn't think you knew it, Frye said to himself.

Then—"Frye! Come on out and we'll talk it over!"

Silence.

"You hear me!"

For a few minutes it was quiet.

"Listen . . . I turned my ankle and can't get out of this goddamn hole!"

Let's see you try, Frye said to himself.

"Come on over and we'll talk this thing out!"

You're doing all right as it is, Frye thought.

Silence again, but suddenly Jordan called, "Frye, you son of a bitch, come on out!"

Frye smiled, thinking: He's getting warmer.

"What kind of a law man are you!"

Silence.

"You're such a brave goddamn law man walk on over here!"

Keep talking, Frye thought.

"Frye . . . I'll make you a bet!"

Silence.

"I'll bet all the money I got you're not man enough to stand up the same time I do!"

What about your ankle?

"You hear me!"

I hear you . . . but I'm not buying in.

"I'm counting three and then standing up!"

Frye looked down the Winchester.

"One!"

Silence.

"Two!"

There was a longer pause.

"Three!"

Frye saw the crown of a hat edge hesitantly above the rocks. He was ready to fire. But the hat tilted awkwardly and he knew it was being held by a stick. His finger relaxed on the trigger.

The hat disappeared.

"You yellow son of a bitch!"

Work yourself up—it went through Frye's mind—till you can't stand any more.

"I gave you credit before . . . but you're nothing but a goddamn woman!"

I hope Dandy Jim can understand some of this, Frye thought.

Now there was a long silence that lasted for the better part of an hour. Then Jordan called for the last time.

"Frye . . . you win! But you're not taking me!"

Silence. Then a single revolver shot.

Frye smiled, hearing the shot die away. Clay, you should have been on the stage.

Throughout the long afternoon there was no sound from the pocket. Frye's eyes stayed on it. He shifted positions as his body became cramped and he smoked cigarettes to help pass the time. As dusk settled, coming quickly between the steep slopes of the valley, he removed his boots, his hat and cartridge belt. Then he cupped his hands to his mouth and whistled the call of a verdin.

He waited until it was darker, then moved on hands and knees a dozen yards to the left and imitated the call again.

Dandy Jim would know that he was moving. And if he was moving it meant only one thing. Close in and get Jordan.

He waited a longer time now, until the moon— what there was of it—appeared above the eastern slope; then Frye began to crawl forward, his Colt in his right hand, watching the rocks ahead of him pale gray in the moonlight.

Thirty yards to go.

All right, let's feel him out. Frye picked up a stone that filled his hand and threw it forward but to the left of Jordan's position.

He heard it strike and instantly the revolver answered.

Frye smiled in the darkness, even though he could feel the tension inside of him. He's good in a saloon fight, he thought, but he's not worth a damn at this. All right. Now you know for sure.

He inched forward a dozen yards and stopped. His hand groped for a stone. Finding one he threw it backhanded toward Jordan.

The stone rattled over the rocks and this time he saw the flame spurt as the revolver went off.

He's not taking any chances.

Now, off beyond Jordan's position he heard the hoot of an owl that he knew was not from an owl. Dandy Jim was closing in. Frye crept forward.

He heard the owl again much closer and this time Jordan's revolver answered it. Frye moved quickly and he reached the rocks that rose in front of the pocket as Jordan's shot echoed to nothing.

Now Frye could hear him: a boot scraped in the loose gravel. He could picture Jordan on the other side of the rock moving around the pocket trying to pierce the darkness, trying to see where they were hiding. Frye pressed close and shifting his Colt to his left hand, edged in that direction along the smooth side of the rock.

If he has one gun there are two bullets left in it. No, he thought then, hurriedly, *you can't count shots. He's had time to reload.*

Wait for Dandy. The next time is the one. In his mind he hesitated and he told himself: *Just do it. Do it and get it the hell over with.*

God . . . help me—

It came suddenly, just beyond the pocket, not an owl sound as he had expected, but the shriek of a coyote, the howl cut off abruptly at its peak as the revolver went off.

Frye moved around the smooth turn of the rock bringing up his Colt.

"Jordan—"

In the moonlight he saw Jordan turning, saw his eyes wide open for a split second before he felt the Colt jump in his hand. Close on the explosion he fired again and five feet away from him Jordan went down, his hands clutched to his face.

Frye called out softly into the darkness, "He's dead," and a moment later Dandy Jim was standing next to him. Frye took Jordan's billfold for identification and gave the dead man's gun and holster to Dandy Jim.

"He died poorly," the Coyotero said strapping it on.

They buried Jordan in the pocket and at first light climbed the slope and ran their horses again the way they had come. It was still the early part of the morning when they descended the slope to the clearing where they had left Danaher. They would water their horses here, then pick up Danaher's sign. But as they crossed the stream they saw Ford Goss standing next to his horse waiting for them.

"You got him?"

Frye nodded. "Last night."

"I'd like to've seen that."

"What about you boys?"

"I came back to find you. We got the others holed up."

"Where?"

"Up a ways. Danaher wanted to wait for you." Ford grinned. "They're hiding up in an old mine works and don't know we know it."

14

From the window of the assay shack, looking down the slope, Tindal could see most of the deserted mine works: the ore tailings, furrowed gravel piles that stretched down the slope in long humps, and just behind the first tailing he could see the top part of the mainshaft scaffolding. Where the ore tailing petered out into the canyon floor he could see the crushing mill and giant cyanide vats, five of them, cradled in a rickety wooden frame.

He remembered the time he had visited here, a guest of—he could not think of the man's first name—something Butler. Butler had lived in Randado and had owned a small interest in the mine. They had not climbed the slope to the assay shack, but had stayed over there across the canyon where the company buildings were: now dilapidated and two of the four were roofless and you could see the framework of studs that the roof planks and tar paper had been nailed to.

The houses were built at the base of the slope and the verandas were supported on stilts. Butler standing on the steps, a cigar in his mouth, explaining the operation—

". . . it's got to be dry-crushed to pass a twenty by sixteen mesh . . . loaded into them vats . . . two hundred and fifty tons of ore, mind you, and leached in cyanide . . . strength of the solution is . . . to the ton of water . . . damn good thing we got water . . . right now the average tenor's thirty dollars to the ton and mister, that's pay dirt!"

It was the first and last time Tindal had visited the mine—"The Big Beverly," they'd called it—for months later the tenor dropped to two dollars and fifty cents a ton and from then on it was not worth working.

The shack he was in right now—

He remembered looking up the slope, up past the cyanide vats and the crushing mill, to the left and even higher than the main shaft scaffolding, and seeing the shack perched on a ledge that was almost halfway up the escarpment. Just sandstone above it; long, towering pinnacles of sandstone.

And Butler saying—". . . why would anybody want to build a shack way up there? Man, that's where the assaying is done. See those two dark spots on either side of the shack . . . the original mine shafts . . . in the shack they got shelves on the walls and bags of concentrates are stored there to be tested . . . you don't want to go up there . . . nothing to see . . . ."

And there's nothing to see looking down from there, Tindal thought now. My God, it's funny what you can remember from even a long time ago. About fifteen years . . . but last week is a long time ago, too. It's how you look at it.

Last week—

Earl Beaudry coming into the store and saying that he'd seen Phil Sundeen and that Phil wanted to talk to them. Why in hell had Earl and George been so eager to stick their noses in another man's business! Sundeen's run-off cows were his own worry. My God, a man can change!

He was thinking of Phil Sundeen then, comparing how he was before with what he was like now. The difference was in Tindal's mind.

He had looked up to Phil Sundeen as everyone did, because Phil was an important man. He had always laughed when Phil started to cut up. When Phil did something that was genuinely funny, Tindal's eyes would water as he laughed and he would feel closer to Phil then, laughing without having to pretend that he was laughing. Those were the times when Tindal would feel justified for all the excuses he continually made for Phil, and the defending him to Milmary, who said he was a rowdy and wouldn't have anything to do with him. "Mil, a man of his stature is entitled to be a little eccentric." "Eccentric! Riding his horse into people's living rooms! Thinking he can do anything he pleases just because he owns a few cows!" "A few thousand." "I don't care how many!" "He's young yet, that's all." "Well, it's about time he grew up!"

He had even made an excuse for Milmary: you can't tell a woman anything. But always in the back of his mind was the hope that someday Milmary would change her attitude and marry Phil. Marrying into the biggest spread in Pima County! For some things it was worth being a little extra nice. Hell, it didn't require much more of an effort. But, my God, the times when you had to laugh and it wasn't funny—

Everything in life isn't a bed of roses. It's just good business to put up with a few minor displeasures in order to make a profit in the end. Once in a while he would view his association with Phil Sundeen this way. Most often though, he would simply justify their association by making excuses for Phil's character. Either way Tindal kept his conscience clean and his pride intact. Doubts did not count.

But now—

Suddenly inside of only a few days there was nothing to gain and everything to lose and he could no longer make excuses for Phil Sundeen. He saw Phil as he actually was, the way Milmary had described him: a rowdy who thinks he can do anything he pleases. He blamed Beaudry and Stedman for getting him into this, but far less than he blamed, and hated, Sundeen now. It would come into his mind: Why can't we just start all over. No, not start over, but go back to the way it was and I swear to God I won't have anything to do with him. The two Mexicans were caught stealing . . . hell, that part's all right. But everything that happened after, Sundeen did. I got no cause to be hiding out. I haven't done anything! And the son of a bitch just sits there like God smoking a cigarette!

He glanced from the window to Sundeen, who was lounging in the open doorway, his back against one side and a booted leg propped up on the other knee. George Stedman was sitting cross-legged against the opposite wall. Stedman's head was down and he was staring at his hands, looking closely at his fingernails clenched against the palm, then with the thumb of the other hand he would work at the dirt wedged beneath the nails.

"Phil."

Sundeen did not look up. He was studying his cigarette, watching the smoke curling from the tip of it.

"Phil," Tindal said again. "Why don't we just go back home and see what happens?" Trying to keep his voice mild it sounded shaky and nervous.

Sundeen's eyes remained on the cigarette, but he said, "I told you to quit that talk."

"We can't stay forever."

"Why not?"

"Phil, we got rights. We don't have to stay out here like hunted animals."

"We do if I say we do."

"You're not being reasonable!"

"Nothing says I have to."

Tindal calmed himself. Getting excited wasn't going to help. "What about your cattle?"

"What about them?"

"You'd let your ranch go just because of this?"

"They know how to graze without my help."

"They'll be scattered all over the territory!"

"Then I'll hire me some men to bring them back."

"When?"

"When I get ready."

"Phil, here's the thing. If we give ourselves up, then Finnerty will let us off for coming in on our own accord."

"Who says so?"

"It stands to reason."

Sundeen looked up now, faintly grinning. "R. D., you old son of a bitch, you telling me we're wrong?"

"I'm facing the facts!"

"Facts don't mean a thing."

"They do when you're faced with them!"

Sundeen's glance went down the slope. "I don't see 'em facing me." He looked at Stedman then. "George, you got any facts facing you?"

Stedman's head jerked up. "What?"

"Phil—"

Sundeen cut him off. "R.D., you're a sad-looking old son of a bitch, but if you don't shut up I'm going to put you out of your misery."

Sundeen stood up stretching, then walked outside and away from the doorway.

Now he's going to look at the horses, Tindal thought. They were kept saddled in one of the old mine shafts that was on the ledge with the assay shack.

He doesn't worry about a solitary thing. Just piddles around like he was at home looking for some trouble to get into. You can see he's restless, but he puts on the act he's having a good time . . . like a spoiled kid who's got to have his own way and even when he's wrong won't admit it. Hell, that's what he is, a snot-nosed kid, who should have had his ass kicked a long time ago.

He glanced at Stedman, then leaned head and shoulders out of the window and looked both ways along the ledge. Sundeen was not in sight.

"George."

Stedman's head lifted and he looked at Tindal almost angrily. "What do you want?"

Tindal glanced at the doorway, then moved closer to Stedman. "George, there must be a way out of this."

"You knew the way in," Stedman said, "you ought to know the way out."

"Me!"

"Who the hell else!"

"Now wait a minute, George. It was you and Earl who got me to talk to Sundeen."

Stedman's eyes narrowed and he said angrily, "You got a short goddamn memory is all I can say."

"You think I'm enjoying this!"

"I don't know why not. Finally you're in something with Phil Sundeen."

"Keep your voice down."

"You don't want him to hear you talking behind his back."

"George, make sense."

"Always shining up to him—"

"Don't talk so loud!"

"Always ready to kiss his hind end any time he bends over."

Tindal shook his head wearily. What was the sense of talking to him.

"Listen." Stedman lowered his voice and the sound of it seemed edged with a threat. "I'm getting out of here. I'm not taking any more off of him; no more of this goddamn obeying orders like we were his hired hands. I'm waiting for the chance and soon as it shows, I'm getting out. You can stay married to the son of a bitch if you want, but I've got a stomach full of him. A man can stand just so much. You wouldn't know about that, would you?"

"What do you mean—"

"Just stay out of my way from now on!"

Tindal felt his temper rise and he was about to curse Stedman and tell him to . . . to do something! But he was too enraged to speak. He turned his back on Stedman and returned to the window.

Imagine him saying that to me. Of all the goddamn spineless, yellow—Tindal gritted his teeth. He'll be sorry. Manager of a bank—If any two-bit illegitimate idiot couldn't be manager of a branch bank! Well, we'll see. We'll get home and see how much business Mr. George S.O.B. Stedman gets after this.

He's so panicky he doesn't even know who to trust. Blames me! He's as bad as Phil. Every bit as crazy!

Like that business with Jordan.

We're not bad off enough, Phil has to get in an argument with Jordan and Jordan leaves. Jordan said it was pointless to come back this way and be hunted like animals—the only one who had anything to say that made sense!

But suddenly Tindal stopped. What was he thinking of? He was reasoning to the point that they *needed* Jordan here. But Jordan wasn't one of

them. Jordan was a gunman, a wanted outlaw, yet
he had been wishing Jordan were here; missing the
secure feeling of having him with them.

My God . . . I think I'm going crazy!

He slumped against the wall and wiped his face
with his bandanna. *Just take it easy. You've gotten
along for forty-five years using your head. Just
calm down. Keep your eyes and ears open, you'll
make out all right.* He looked across the room at
Stedman. *George can go take a running jump to
hell . . . and take Phil with him.*

He had made himself become calm and now he
sucked at his teeth, the first time he had done this in
five days.

Sundeen appeared in the doorway, unexpectedly,
and Tindal felt himself straighten against the wall.
Sundeen hesitated, looking from Tindal to Stedman, then said, as if reluctantly, "They're coming."

"Where!" Stedman was scrambling to his feet as
he said it.

"Just stay where you are!" Sundeen was inside
the doorway now looking past the frame. He was
silent, then said, "They're coming up the road, just
entering the canyon."

Stedman moved toward the window and Sundeen snapped, "I said stay where you are!"

Against the wall next to the window, Tindal
could see them now straggling in almost single file.

The first ones were reaching the company buildings now.

He heard Sundeen go over to the shelf along this side wall where his blankets were and slip his rifle out from between them.

Then another sound—

He looked back to see Stedman reaching the door and going out, stumbling as he started down the slope, then regaining his feet and running, sliding in the loose sand, shouting something to the men below—

15

In the directly above them sunlight of noon they entered the widening in the canyon that was the site of the mine. Frye and Danaher rode side by side a dozen lengths behind Merl White. The others were strung out behind them. Farther back, where there had been rock slides, the canyon was narrow and they had thinned out single file to pass through and had not closed up again before reaching the mine.

The day before they had followed the tracks up the canyon and spent the night a mile below the mine site. But before dark Merl had gone on alone to study the deserted building through Danaher's glasses. Just before dark closed in he saw the figure up by the assay shack. That was it. They would wait until morning to go in. It was Danaher who added that they would also wait for Frye. It was Frye's party.

Frye saw Merl White dismount in front of one of the company buildings and tie his reins to one of the support posts beneath the veranda. They can't be too close, Frye thought. His eyes moved across the open area to the mine works, then lifted to the sandstone escarpment high above. He thought: Where would you hide?

"John, where are they?"

Danaher nodded, looking up the slope. "That shack way up there. They used to use it for assaying."

"I was wondering about us just walking in."

"We're out of range."

"Unless Phil's a dead-eye."

"Three hundred yards is long for anybody."

"Maybe they sneaked out during the night," Frye said.

"Merl was here with the sun this morning," Danaher answered. "He saw movement up by the shack."

Merl White had the glasses to his eyes, now standing at the edge of the veranda shade studying the assay shack. They were up there and they might as well realize they were trapped. Maybe they would give themselves up and nobody would be hurt. Maybe. The trouble was you could not count on Sundeen to use reason.

"Look!" Merl shouted it without taking the glasses from his eyes. "Coming out of the shack!"

They could not see him at first, not until he came off the ledge and started down, a dark speck against the sand-colored slope, then dust rising in a cloud behind him. They saw him roll and slide head first and for a moment he was hidden by the dust. Then, on his feet again, running, pumping his legs to keep up with his momentum.

A rifle shot cracked in the stillness and echoed thinly in the wide canyon. Then another and another and puffs of sand chased the running figure down the slope.

Three shots before the men below had their rifles out of saddle boots, before they were scattering but moving their horses toward the slope to return the fire—aiming at the shack to cover the man coming down.

Then he was past the cyanide vats, swerving to find cover behind the massive structure, and the firing stopped.

Frye's men walked their horses back toward the company building where Frye and Danaher stood with Merl White as the man came across the open area toward them—every few steps looking back over his shoulder, up toward the assay shack.

Then as he became aware of the silent, grim-faced men waiting for him, he seemed to hesitate, walking more slowly now and he began to brush the sand from his clothes. He was breathing heavily and his face, gray with dust, bore a pained expression.

"I'm giving myself up," Stedman gasped.

No one spoke.

His eyes, suddenly wide open, went over the line

of men, hesitating on Haig Hanasian before they came to rest on Frye.

"Kirby, I've wanted to give myself up . . . I couldn't with that madman!" He looked at Danaher, then back to Frye, waiting for one of them to speak. "I pleaded with him . . . I said, 'Phil, let's go on home and face up to it.' I tried everything humanly possible, but he'd just grin or else start cursing and there was nothing I could do about it."

Frye stepped toward him. "That's all right, Mr. Stedman." He opened Stedman's coat almost gently and saw that he was not armed. "You come on in here," Frye said, taking his arm, "in the shade and sit down."

"Kirby," Stedman murmured, "the man's crazy."

Frye nodded leading him by the arm under the veranda. "How many are up there now, Mr. Stedman, just the two of them?"

"Phil and R. D."

"How's Mr. Tindal doing?"

Stedman hesitated, but he said, "He's all right."

"Did Phil harm either of you?"

"He like to drove us out of our mind." Stedman was perspiring and his fingers pulled at his collar loosening it.

"Did he harm you?"

"Not like you probably mean."

"Or Mr. Tindal?"

"No . . . but you never know what he'll do. He picked a fight with Jordan. But Jordan had a gun. He wouldn't take any of Phil's airs and he left." Stedman added almost grudgingly, "He was smart to get out while he could."

Frye nodded, "Yes sir," and asked, "how are Phil's supplies?"

"Water and food for two days. No, that was for three of us. They could make what they have go four or five days if they had to."

"You said Mr. Tindal's all right?"

Stedman nodded. "He's all right."

"How do they get along?"

Stedman was calmer now and he said, "They quit sleeping together," and grinned. But he saw Danaher's cold stare and looking back at Frye he explained, "They're not getting along. But R. D.'s too goddamn scared to do anything about it."

Danaher smiled. "Not the man of action you are, George."

"Well, I thought why should I sit up there and—"

"Shut up!" Contempt was in Danaher's eyes and in his voice when he said, "Prisoners speak when they're asked a question. No other time!"

Frye said, "Sit down for a while, Mr. Stedman," and turned following Danaher out into the sunlight. Frye made a cigarette and stood next to Danaher looking up at the assay shack.

"That's a long open stretch up that slope," Frye said after a minute.

Danaher nodded. "Going up the off side of those ore tails we'd be covered all the way up to the ledge. But you still have to go in the front door of the shack once you get there."

Frye was looking at the sandstone heights that towered above the shack. "Phil might be just the one to try climbing his way out."

"He might at that," Danaher said. "But it would have to be at night else we could run up close and knock him off."

"If he wanted to do it," Frye said, "Phil wouldn't let a little thing like nighttime stop him."

"Well, we better have somebody get around there," Danaher said. "It would probably take a while."

Frye called over Dandy Jim and told him what they had been talking about. The Coyotero looked up at the heights, picturing the country behind it and the roundabout trail it would take to reach it, and then he told that it would be near dark by the time a man arrived there.

Yes, he would be willing to go. Merl White agreed, and when he volunteered so did Goss and Tobin and in less than ten minutes the four of them were riding back down the canyon.

"That," Danaher said, "closes the back door."

"But there're two side doors," Frye said, meaning up and down the canyon. His eyes roamed over the deserted mine works. "And enough good places to hide right here in the house."

"Well, Kirby, that just takes it out of the commonplace."

He looked at Danaher. "I think you're enjoying this."

"Kirby, if I didn't like my job I'd get the hell out."

"I can't picture you in anything else."

"Which makes it all the easier." Danaher said then, "Aren't you having a good time?"

"I don't know if you'd call it that."

"Would you rather be back trading horses?"

Frye shook his head. "No."

"Then get to work and figure a way to pry that crazy bastard out of there."

"We might go up and talk to him," Frye said. "Maybe he's calmed down. Take a white flag to show we're friendly."

Danaher thought about it before nodding. "So we can say we tried." He took a handkerchief from his pocket and smoothed it out before tying it to the end of his Henry rifle.

Frye leaned his carbine against a support post and they started across the open area, Danaher motioning his men to follow. When they had crossed to the cyanide vats, the sheriff motioned again.

They strung out in a line, their rifles ready, as Frye and Danaher started up the slope.

They kept their eyes on the shack, going up slowly in the shifting sand, climbing abreast but with a few yards separating them. The shack seemed deserted: the boards bleached gray by years of sun and wind and there was not a sign of life in the dark opening of the doorway or in the windows.

They were fifty yards up the slope—

"If he doesn't show in the next minute"— Danaher's breathing was labored—"we're gettin' the hell back."

Frye's eyes remained on the shack. "What would you give to know what he's thinking?"

The answer came from the shack. On top of Frye's question the rifle shot whined down kicking up sand almost directly between them. Danaher's men were ready; they began firing, keeping it up as Frye and Danaher dove in opposite directions and rolled. Danaher came up firing the Henry, then turned and ran. As they reached the bottom of the slope the firing stopped.

Walking back, Frye said, "Now we know what George felt like."

Danaher was untying the white cloth. "I burned my best handkerchief."

"That's what you get for carrying a live truce flag."

Danaher grumbled something, then looking back

up the slope he said, "With a clean conscience, Kirby, we can say we tried. Now we sit back and wait for Mr. Sundeen."

"And judging by his short patience," Frye answered, "that shouldn't be too long a wait."

Haig Hanasian warmed up their meat and made coffee on the stove inside the company building. The stove was almost beyond use and there was no stack on it to take out the smoke, but it didn't matter because they ate their meal outside under the veranda, watching the assay shack. Through the afternoon they played poker with matchsticks for chips or just sat smoking and talking, waiting for something that they knew would come sooner or later. As darkness settled they moved across the open area and paired off taking up positions along the base of the slope, then settled down again to wait. By Danaher's timepiece it was a little after eight o'clock. Haig Hanasian was told to remain at the company building and watch Stedman. It was to keep him out of the way. They knew Stedman would not try to escape.

At ten, Danaher ground the stub of his cigar into the sand, handed his timepiece to Frye, and rolled up in his blankets to sleep. Frye would watch the first part of the night; Danaher would then be up until daylight. He had instructed his men to do it the same way.

Frye sat in the darkness listening to the wind

high up the canyon. It would moan softly, then rise
to a dull hissing sound and he would hear the sand
being blown against the deserted buildings. It kept
going through his mind: What would you do if you
were Phil Sundeen?

He smoked cigarettes thinking about Tindal up
there with him; and from Tindal his thoughts went
to Milmary. What would Mil be doing right now?
He would light a cigarette and as the match flared
look to see what time it was.

Eleven o'clock passed. Then twelve.

It was shortly before one (the way he figured it
later) when he heard the revolver shot from up on
the slope, and the first thing he thought of was
Jordan—

Twice in two days!

Danaher was up, shaking off his blankets. Wide
awake.

"What is it!"

Frye was standing now looking up the dark
slope. The moon was behind the clouds and he
could see nothing. "Up there, John!"

"That was a shot, wasn't it?"

"A handgun."

In the stillness they heard one of the men down
from them lever a shell into his rifle.

"John . . . Jordan pulled one that could be just
like this."

"What?"

They heard a voice calling from up on the slope and there was no time to explain.

Then the sound of the voice came to them clearly—

"He's dead!"

Still they could not see him, but now they knew it was Tindal standing out in front of the shack.

"He shot himself!" The voice echoed in the canyon.

Momentarily there was silence.

"John, it could be a trick."

Danaher cupped his hands to his mouth. "Tindal, you come down!" To Frye he said, "Let's get him out of the way first."

"I can't!"

"I said come down!"

"I can't!" It came as a hoarse scream.

"We better go up," Danaher said. He waved to the men over on his right to start up the slope.

"John—" Frye hesitated. "Something's wrong."

They heard Tindal scream again, "He's dead!"

Danaher called again, "I said come down!"

"I can't!"

Danaher was suddenly at the end of his patience. He said roughly, "Come on!" and started up the slope.

Frye looked to the left, toward two of the men. He ran a few steps toward them. "One of you stay down . . . keep your eyes open!" then turned going up the slope after Danaher. The other man followed him.

Halfway up Danaher called, "Tindal!"

No answer.

Danaher muttered, "Damn him—"

They could make out the ledge now as the clouds passed from in front of the moon and suddenly Tindal was screaming again—

"He's getting away!"

They heard the muffled sound of hoofs somewhere off to the left.

"He's getting away! Stop him!"

The horse whinnied, over beyond the hump of the ore tailing closest to them.

"Phil's getting away!"

Danaher bellowed, "Shut up goddamn-it!"

He wheeled then, almost sliding in the sand, and called down to his men below, "Get him!"

Now they were running down the slope as firing broke suddenly from below—three shots . . . a fourth. Then the firing and the echoes of it dissolved to nothing and in the stillness they could hear the hoofbeats of the horse dying away up canyon.

They knew without going any farther. Sundeen had gotten away.

16

Now there was nothing they could do until morning.

They waited for Tindal to come down and he described what had happened as they walked back to the company building.

Sundeen had fired the revolver shot, he told excitedly, then had made him yell out that he was dead. "He had to get you all part of the way up the slope before he could make a break. He led one of the horses out of the mine entrance, then held his gun on me while I yelled . . . that's why I couldn't move. He'd a cut me down!"

As they brought Tindal under the veranda they heard three shots spaced apart and sounding far off, coming from beyond the escarpment.

"That's the others," Frye said.

He walked out to the middle of the open area leading his horse. Then he fired three shots into the air at ten-second intervals. That would tell the Coyotero there was no hurry. Then he mounted and rode up canyon almost half a mile and fired three

times again. That would be the direction they
would take. He knew the Coyotero would understand. If there was no hurry then they would leave
in the morning, traveling up canyon.

He returned to the men in front of the company
building after unsaddling and picketing his horse—
cigarette glows in the darkness and low murmurs
of sound as they talked about what had happened.
He saw Tindal sitting against the wall next to Stedman, neither of them talking, and Haig Hanasian
standing over them. Danaher stood off by himself
near the end of the veranda.

He thinks it's his fault, Frye thought. Well, let
him be. Don't interrupt a man when he's giving
himself hell.

With first light they were saddled and making
their way up canyon. The sandstone walls seemed
to shrink and become narrower as they followed
the road that was almost overgrown with brush
and in less than an hour they were out of the
canyon, descending a long sweeping meadow toward distant timber. Coming out of the rocks they
saw riders far off to the right following an arroyo
down out of the high country and by the time they
reached the timber they were joined by Dandy Jim,
Merl White, Goss and Tobin.

Merl White said, "What's the matter with you
boys letting one get away?" then shut up as he saw
the look on Danaher's face.

Frye explained to him what had taken place. Then— "He angled across the meadow and right into the timber, Merl. That's almost due west. If he keeps going he'll run right into Sun-D land."

Merl nodded. "If I was him I'd at least want to take a look around home."

"It makes sense," Frye said.

"Well, let's go then."

"We got something else for you, Merl."

"What?"

"Taking these two into Randado."

"Not me."

"You and Ford and Joe's been riding longer than the rest of us."

"We got more of a reason to, Kirby; outside of you. Get somebody else to do it."

There was no sense in arguing it. Frye asked two of Danaher's men and they said they would, gladly in fact. He told Haig that he could go in also, but Haig shook his head and stated that he would rather stay out.

Before separating, Frye moved his gelding next to one of the men who was going back.

"Don't put them in jail."

"Why not?"

"They won't be going anywhere."

Danaher's man shrugged. "It don't matter to me."

Now they rode on toward Sun-D, watching the

four horses move off, more to the southwest, toward Randado.

When they came out of the timber Danaher pulled his horse closer to Frye's. For a while they rode along in silence, but Frye knew what was coming.

Finally—

"Kirby, that was my fault he got away."

"No, you can't take the blame for something like that."

"I got impatient."

"Well, you were anxious."

"I got to learn to hold on to myself more."

"You been doing all right for forty years."

Danaher seemed not to hear. "Like with Digo . . . I beat the hell out of him and nothing happens. You whisper something in his ear and he runs off at the mouth."

Frye felt embarrassed for Danaher and he wished that he would stop talking this way. It seemed out of character, not like the rough-voiced, coarse-featured Sheriff of Pima County. But that was Danaher. He was man enough to admit when he was wrong, even if it made him feel like a fool to do it.

"John, why don't we just forget about it?"

"I intend to," Danaher said. "I just wanted to make it clear that it was my fault he got away."

And that was the end of it. After that, Danaher was himself again.

Within two hours they had crossed the eastern boundary of Sun-D land and an hour and a half later they were in sight of the ranch house and its outbuildings.

They pulled up in a mesquite thicket a hundred yards behind the main building, then waited while Merl, Ford and Joe went on, keeping to the brush, until they were beyond the bunkhouse and corral. They saw Merl come out of the mesquite far down and as he did, they rode toward the ranch house, splitting as they reached it, circling around both sides of the house to meet in the yard. They saw Merl and his two riders come around the corner of the bunkhouse.

A dog barked and came running toward them from the barn. The dog stopped, cocking his head to look at them, then went over to Merl as he dismounted and sniffed his boots. Merl reached down to pat him, then came up drawing his carbine from the scabbard. He looked at Frye, who was dismounted now, and Frye nodded toward the bunkhouse.

They heard the screen door of the ranch house open and close. A Mexican woman came out to the edge of the veranda.

Merl called, "That's Digo's woman."

Frye walked toward her touching his hand to the brim of his hat and he said in Spanish, "We are looking for the younger Sundeen."

"He isn't here," the woman said.

"When did he leave?"

"Days ago."

"His father is here?"

"He is ill."

"We won't disturb him . . . only long enough for a few words."

The woman shrugged and moved aside, but as Frye stepped up on the porch, Danaher and Haig Hanasian following him, she asked suddenly, "Where is Digo?"

"He is in jail."

The woman seemed to relax. "For how long?"

"It's not for me to say."

"Will they hang him?"

"No."

The woman half turned from them touching her breast and closing her eyes as they went inside.

"Who is it?"

They looked toward the sofa that was placed at a right angle from the stone fireplace. Phil Sundeen's father was lying there, a quilt covering him and a pillow at one end holding up his head. His face was still leathery brown, but the skin sagged from his cheekbones and his eyes, lusterless, were half closed. Frye would not have recognized him. He remembered Old Val as a robust, swaggering man always with a cigar clamped between the hard lines of his jaw, and with thick graying hair that always seemed to have a line around it where his hat fitted. Frey remembered that clearly.

They walked toward him and he said again, "Who is it?"

"Val, this is John Danaher."

His eyes opened all the way. "What do you want?"

"This is Kirby Frye. . . . He used to work for you about ten years ago."

"I don't place the name." The old man's voice was hard, but with little volume.

"Mr. Sundeen," Frye said, "I'm sorry you're laid up."

"If you want a job you'll have to see Phil. I don't hire no more."

"No sir. I didn't come for a job."

Danaher said, "Val, that's who we're looking for. Phil."

"You try De Spain's?"

"Not yet. We thought we'd try here first."

"He might give the boy a job, I don't know."

"Val, was he here this morning?"

"I remember now we lost some boys a few days ago, so maybe Phil'll be hiring again."

Danaher exhaled slowly. "You didn't see him this morning?"

"I don't know if it was this morning or yesterday."

"Val, just try to think a minute. He stopped in here this morning to talk to you."

The old man's head nodded. "I think he did."

"Did he tell you what happened?"

"He didn't say anything about hiring any more men."

Danaher exhaled again. "Did he say where he was going?"

"But if he was going to hire men, he'd a told where he'd be, so I could send 'em to him."

Frye glanced at Danaher, then kneeled on one knee next to the sofa.

"Mr. Sundeen, I certainly admired working for you that time. The first year we pushed 'em all the way up to Ellsworth. You remember that?"

"Two thousand head," the old man murmured.

"Then the next year we went to McDowell and San Carlos and you let Phil trail-boss the bunch to the reservation."

The old man's eyes rolled to look at Frye. "I don't remember you. You see Phil, though, tell him I said it's all right to hire you."

"Well, I sure wish I could find him."

"You got to know where to look."

"Where do you start?"

"When I wanted Phil I looked where there was women. That's where I'd start and that's where I'd end."

"Maybe that's the thing to do."

"Hell yes it is. Phil's got a nose for women. He can smell 'em." The old man's mouth formed a weak smile. "Like a hound dog in heat, only Phil's like it all year round. I used to say, 'Phil, for cry-sake get yourself a woman and bring her home and be done with it. You'll wear out your seat ridin' to town every night.' And he used to say, 'I'll wear out more'n that,' and just laugh."

Frye said, "He's something."

"You looking for Phil? Go ask the women. They'll tell you where he's at." Old Val chuckled.

"Would you look any place in particular?"

"You want a job pretty bad, don't you?"

"Well I'd sure like to find Phil."

"Once he said, 'Why in hell does a man get married with all the women there are in the world just beggin' for it?' And I said, 'Son, when they're beg-gin' you ain't wantin' and when you're wantin' they ain't beggin'. That's why you got to have your-self one handy.' "

Frye said, "Yes sir."

"Are you married, boy?"

"No sir, I'm not."

"Do you want to?"

"I think so."

"Well, it'll be a long way off. Phil don't pay more'n forty a month to top hands." The old man grinned. "And you sure don't want to take your wife in the bunkhouse."

"Mr. Sundeen, I better try and catch up with Phil."

"Phil don't poke along. You'll have to move."

"But you're sure he was here this morning."

"A man's a fool to say he's absolutely sure about anything."

"He might have been here then."

"He might have been."

Frye rose. "Maybe we'll talk again some time soon, Mr. Sundeen."

The old man rolled his eyes and Frye could see the yellowish cast to them as he looked up. "You better make it soon if you've got anything to say."

Frye nodded. "Yes sir." He turned and followed Danaher outside to the porch. Then he stopped, looking out to the yard seeing Merl and the others standing by the horses. He glanced back at the screen door, then at Danaher.

"John, what happened to Haig?"

Danaher looked toward the horses. Haig's was not there. "I don't know. He walked out while you were talking." He called over to Merl, "Where's Haig?"

"He rode off," Merl answered. "Didn't say a word, just rode off."

17

Sundeen waited in the shadow of the adobe wall
until the wagon started down the alley, moving
away from the Metropolitan Café, then he crossed
the alley to the stairway that slanted up to the back
porch.

He had left his horse in the thicket that bordered
Randado's small Mexican community and had
crept from one adobe to the next, keeping close to
the walls, occasionally hearing siesta hour snoring
coming from within, until he reached the alley that
was in back of the café. The wagon had been a
small delay, already unloaded when he reached the
last adobe wall.

Now he hesitated before going up the stairs. He
moved to the wall next to the back window and
looked into the kitchen. Noontime activity. The
cook facing the stove, a waitress just pushing
through the door to go out front. The door swung
back and Edith Hanasian came in with it. She was
looking in his direction, but did not see him and he
thought: Call her now! But she turned toward the

stove, saying something to the cook, and it occurred to him: No. Wait a while, till the rush is over. He was tired, dust-caked and wanted a drink. The best thing would be to go upstairs and wait for her. Have a drink and take a load off your feet, he decided.

He climbed the stairs and went inside, following the hallway to the living room at the front. He took off his hat and coat, dropping them on the floor, and sank down into a stuffed leather chair stretching his long legs out in front of him. But he had forgotten the drink.

Phil pulled himself up and went down the hall to Edith's bedroom. He went directly to her dresser and lifted the half-full bottle of whisky from the lower right-hand drawer, then returned to the easy chair.

For some time he sat in the chair, his head low on the bolster, and drank from the bottle. Then he placed it on the floor next to him and made a cigarette.

He felt pretty good now even though his legs were stiff and he had a kink in his back from all that riding. He felt good enough to grin as he thought: Damn room looks different in the daylight.

He thought of Edith then and wished she would hurry up and get finished with the dinner trade. Won't she be surprised! He laughed out loud.

I'll tell her I saw little Haig.

Edith, I think that little hairy-faced husband of yours is quit the restaurant business and taken to mining. Him and some others were looking over that Big Beverly claim in the Huachucas yesterday. Edith, why else you suppose he'd be snooping around over there? Phil laughed again and took another pull at the bottle.

About Haig Hanasian, Phil had no feeling one way or the other. He was indifferent to him, as he was about most things. If a man couldn't hold on to his wife, that was too bad. He shouldn't have married her to begin with. If Edith wanted to fool around that was Haig's own fault. Hell, he got her through a Prescott marriage broker. Edith had admitted that much herself.

He remembered when Haig had come here to open his café, bringing Edith with him. There had been a lot of talk about them then, but Phil had never been too interested in the talk; he had just watched Edith, waiting to catch her eye as she served him, and when their eyes would meet he would tell her things without even opening his mouth. He never forced his attention on her. He didn't have to. To Phil it seemed the most natural thing in the world that she should want him; if anything, he considered that he was doing her a favor.

What fun would she get out of Haig? What was he, a Greek? No . . . something that sounded like ammonia. Well, he looked like a goddamn Greek. Came over on a boat and opened a restaurant in New Orleans; then packed up and came out here. Probably his health. Or maybe they wanted to send him back where he came from, so he ran.

Haig had gone to Prescott first. He traveled through the whole southern part of the territory until deciding to locate in Randado. Then he returned to Prescott to find a wife.

Edith told Phil she had come from San Francisco to marry a soldier in Whipple Barracks, but he had died while she was on the way. Killed in action against the Apaches. She would lower her eyes telling it. To Phil, that was as good a story as any; but he always had the suspicion that the Prescott marriage broker had to raid a whorehouse to fill Haig's order. One way or another, it didn't matter to Phil.

As soon as he saw Haig at the mine he had thought about coming here. Habit, he thought grinning. That comes from duckin' up the stairs every time you see him ride out.

Then when he arrived at the ranch and did not find Digo, he was sure he would come here. Digo's wife did not know where he was; but Edith would know. Only now was the awareness that he was alone beginning to take hold of him. He had been alone from the start. Tindal and Stedman and Jordan had never been a consolation, only company; company he had to force to stay with him, and now he did not even have that.

As soon as he found Digo everything would be all right. Hell, it wasn't any fun playing this game by yourself. Digo would have some ideas. Probably he's out looking for me. But he'd have left word with Edith so we could meet in case I came back.

With Phil it was that simple. This was something to do; something to relieve the boredom of tending cows all year long. But with Digo along it would be a hell of a lot more fun.

Only occasionally during the last few days did he try to think what the outcome of this might be; and always he had gotten it out of his mind by thinking of an immediate concern. Hell, don't worry about tomorrow. It might not even come.

But just since this morning, since not finding Digo at the ranch, it had crept into his mind more often: How is this thing going to end? And what seemed more important: What if I don't find Digo?

But now he had whisky, and he was relaxed.

He had almost finished the bottle when Edith came in.

Surprise showed on her face momentarily, but it vanished as she glanced from Phil to the whisky bottle on the floor next to him.

"Why don't you help yourself to a drink, Phil?"

Sundeen grinned. "Edith, you're somethin'."

"When did you get in?"

"About an hour ago."

"Alone?"

"All by myself."

"What happened to your friends?"

"They got sick and went home."

"Somebody said Tindal and Stedman were brought in, but I didn't see them." She was silent, watching him grinning looking up at her. "What do you want, Phil?"

"I didn't come for a haircut." He winked at her.

"You could use one."

Sundeen laughed. "For a woman affectionate as you are you can sure act cold."

"What do you want, Phil?"

Sundeen's expression changed. "Edith, you sound funny."

"I'm not used to having wanted outlaws in my living room."

He straightened in the chair and his mouth came open in surprise as he stared at her. "Well god-*damn* . . . ain't we somethin' all of a sudden!"

"Why don't you just get out?"

He came up out of the chair suddenly taking her by the shoulders. "What's the matter with you!"

"Let me go!"

"You think I came to see *you!*"

"Take your hands off of me!"

He shook her violently. "You think I came for you!"

"I don't care why you came!"

He threw her away from him and shook his head slowly, saying, "Son of a bitch," spacing the words. "When I learn to figure out women then I'll be the smartest man walking this earth!"

She asked hesitantly, "Why did you come?"

"To find Digo. God almighty, not to see you!"

Edith smiled faintly as if taking pleasure in saying, "He's across the street."

"Where across the street?"

Edith moved to the window and pointed out. "Right over there. They call it the jail."

"What!"

"Take the wax out of your ears—I said he's in jail!"

Sundeen went to the next window and pushed the curtain aside roughly.

"When'd they get him?"

"The same day you left."

"You're sure?" He kept staring at the front of the jail.

"I saw them take him inside," Edith said calmly. "I haven't seen him come out."

"Edith, if you're pullin' a joke—"

She smiled. "What will you do, Phil?"

Sundeen did not answer her. The side of his face

was pressed against the glass pane and he was looking down the street. Edith studied him for a moment not understanding, then she moved closer to
the window and looked in the same direction. She
saw then, halfway down the block, Frye and Danaher riding side by side and a line of riders strung out
behind them.

"Mr. Sundeen—"

Edith heard the voice behind her, recognizing it,
seeing Haig even before she turned. Phil wheeled,
drawing his gun, and stopped dead seeing Haig
Hanasian standing in the door. He carried a rifle in
the crook of his arm, but it was pointed to the floor.

"Your father said I might find you here," Haig
said.

"What? He didn't even know I was home."

"You don't know your father."

"Haig, do you aim to use that rifle?"

"Why should I?"

"Then set it against the wall." Sundeen grinned.
"I thought you had designs of using it on me."

"Not now," Haig said quietly.

Edith moved toward him hesitantly. "How long
have you been here?"

"For a few minutes," Haig said. "I believe I came
in when you were reminding Mr. Sundeen that you
weren't used to having outlaws in the living room."

"Oh—"

"I agree, Edith."

She looked at him surprised, then dropped her eyes again.

Sundeen shook his head. "I feel sorry for you, brother."

"I think you're the one to feel sorry for," Haig said.

"Why?"

"You're all alone. Now you have to run all by yourself."

And as if this brought it back to mind, he said, angrily, "Where's Digo?"

"He's in jail."

"He can't be."

Haig shrugged. "Go see for yourself." He watched Sundeen go to the window, then turn from it abruptly and start to make a cigarette. His fingers seemed clumsy and rolling it he tore the paper, spilling the tobacco. He threw the shreds of it to the floor and walked over to the whisky bottle.

"That Frye—" he mumbled. He picked up the bottle and drank from it. "That goddamn Frye . . . he's the one—" He sank into the chair then and hunched over, leaning on his knees holding the bottle between them, and for a time he seemed deep in thought and did not speak.

He took another drink. Frye was the one. Frye started it. A kid who thinks he's something. Well maybe we ought to show this kid. Maybe we ought

mtion by Gila. The decline permanently involved—
battle. Mount the McLean gun-lance and by
(adobe—were down in Old Mexico taking part in
an adventure that would dramatically change them
elves and whereabouts, lead to the Big Showdown
known or more as The Rincon Mountains.

taken by C. S. Fly, the five principals involved—
Early, Moon, the McKean girl, Loco and Bo
Catlett—were down in Old Mexico taking part in
an adventure that would dramatically change their
lives and, subsequently, lead to the Big Shootout
known by most as The Rincon Mountain War.

to throw it in his face and see what kind of a man he is—

What're you doing runnin' from a kid!

And suddenly it was no longer a game.

He stood up, looking at Haig. "You get ahold of this Frye. Tell him I'll be in De Spain's. Tell him in front of everybody I want to see him there . . . and if he says he won't come, tell him then he better ride out of Randado before the hour's up else I'll gun him the hell out!"

18

As they entered the street, Danaher sidestepped his chestnut closer to Frye's dun. "Are your friends in jail?"

Frye glanced at him questioningly.

"Tindal and Stedman," Danaher said.

Frye shook his head. "No."

"I didn't think so."

"I didn't see any reason for it. I told your man to let them go home."

"You didn't see any reason for it once before."

Frye grinned. He was tired, but relaxed, and for a while he had even stopped thinking of Sundeen. He was looking forward to a good meal and a bed with sheets. After that he would start worrying about Sundeen again. He'd send wires to every major town in the Territory. Never finding him would be just as good, perhaps better than bringing him back. Frye sat in the saddle loosely following the walking motion of the horse. It felt good for a change not to be sitting on the edge of his nerves.

"I think they've had enough punishment for

right now," he said to Danaher, "without being locked up."

Danaher shrugged. "They're your prisoners." He said then, "That reminds me, what are you going to do with Dandy Jim?"

"I'll have to hand him over to the Army."

"What was he doing, just drinking tulapai?"

"That's all, though he caught his wife with somebody while he was drunk and fixed up her face."

"They don't care about things like that," Danaher said. "Somebody will give him a lecture on the evils of tulapai and that'll be the end of it."

Along both sides of the street now Frye saw people stopping and turning to watch them ride by. Some of them waved; a few called out a welcome and he heard Danaher say, "They're a little friendlier this time."

Frye nodded thinking of the morning they had brought in Earl Beaudry.

"Maybe letting Tindal and Stedman go was a good idea after all," Danaher said pleasantly. "Now all you have to do is nail Sundeen's ears to the door and you'll have their respect."

There were more men under the wooden awning at De Spain's. A hand went up here and there and Frye nodded to them. He was reining toward the jail when he saw Milmary Tindal standing in front of the store. She was watching him, her eyes remaining on him even as he returned her stare.

Go on in the jail, he thought. You don't owe her anything. Let her wait a little bit if she's got something to say. But he hesitated. What good would that do? He flicked his reins back again and turned away from Danaher, urging his gelding toward her now.

She looked up at him and for a moment neither of them spoke. Then he said, "Mil," and stepped out of the saddle.

"Are you back for good, Kirby?"

"I don't know. We didn't get Sundeen."

"Maybe he'll turn himself in now."

"Maybe."

She hesitated, not knowing what to say, and her eyes left his.

"How's your father?"

She looked at him again. "Fine. He's resting. Kirby . . . we appreciate you not holding him in jail."

"That's all right."

"Mama says he must've lost ten pounds." She smiled and said this as if to make all of what had happened seem light and of little importance.

"He might've at that," Frye said.

She hesitated again and for a moment neither of them spoke.

"Mil . . . I thought I'd call on you this evening."

She smiled. "That would be fine, Kirby."

He could see relief in her eyes and she looked suddenly as if she might cry.

"Why don't we have supper together?" he said.

"All right—"

"Call for you at the store?"

"Fine, Kirby."

He smiled at her, then turned away leading his gelding across the street. They'd have a long talk tonight; and in the darkness it would be easier for both of them.

Harold Mendez opened the door for him, stepping aside as Frye entered. Danaher was seated, swiveled around with his back to the desk.

"Everything all right, Kirby?"

Frye nodded. "It'll take a few days to get back to normal."

Harold Mendez said, "Everybody's talking about you letting Tindal and Stedman go."

"They still have to face the judge," Frye said.

"But you *could* keep them locked up," Harold said. "That's what they're talking about." Harold's gaze went to the open door, then shifted quickly to Danaher. "I thought you said Haig had disappeared?"

"He did," Danaher said.

"He's coming across the street."

Frye turned to the window and Danaher came out of the chair.

Suddenly Harold said, "My God . . . look!"

De Spain's doors were open and men were hurrying out, separating both ways along the adobe fronts, but most of them coming out to the street, then stopping to look back at De Spain's. They were forming groups, talking, still keeping their eyes on the open doors. A man came out of the Metropolitan and called something and from the crowd someone called back to him, "Sundeen—"

Now Haig Hanasian came into the jail office. His eyes sought out Frye.

"Did you hear?"

"You mean he's in De Spain's?"

Haig nodded. "I have a message from him. He wants you to meet him inside."

"You were talking to him?"

"For a few minutes. He came to find Digo."

"Where?"

"In my living room."

"Oh—"

"He was talking to my wife."

Frye said quickly, "He came to find Digo and when you told him he's in jail he asked for me?"

Haig nodded. "I think he finally realizes this is not a game . . . and he holds you responsible for what has happened. I think he enjoyed it when he had others with him, but now he is alone."

"No, it's not a game," Danaher said mildly. He

went to the gun rack and took down a Henry. "I'll round up the others."

Frye hesitated. "John, I better do this myself."

"You don't get extra pay doing it alone."

"He's calling me."

"All right, you'll show with a full house."

"Remember, you said before I'd have to nail his ears to the door to get everybody's respect."

"I was just talking. What you did to Clay Jordan is enough. After that spreads around you're good here for life."

"John, I'm going over to talk to him."

Danaher studied his deputy. He took a cigar from his breast pocket and bit the tip off. "Kirby, as far as I'm concerned you've got nothing to prove. Phil's crazy enough to start shooting." Danaher hesitated. "It wouldn't be worth it."

"He'd like to back me down," Frye said. "Just to look good one last time."

"Taking men with you isn't backing down," Danaher insisted.

"It would be to Phil," Frye said. "And it might be to all those people outside."

Harold Mendez said, "The hell with them."

"It's not that easy," Frye said.

Harold shrugged. "It's as easy as you want to make it."

Frye started for the door and Danaher said

quickly, "Kirby, he doesn't use his head. You watch his gun now!"

"I will, John."

He was outside then, going down the three steps and the men in the street were turning to look at him, those in his way stepping aside as he started across. He saw Milmary in front of the Metropolitan and he looked away from her quickly, his eyes returning to the dark square of De Spain's open doorway.

His right hand hung at his side as he stepped up onto the porch and he felt his thumb brush the grip of the Colt. Take it slow, he thought. Don't try to read his mind.

He walked into the dimness of De Spain's.

Phil Sundeen stood three quarters of the way down the bar. He was facing the front, his left elbow on the edge of the bar and a three-ounce whisky glass was in his hand held waist high. His eyes stayed with Frye.

Behind the bar, De Spain waited until Frye stopped, ten feet separating him from Sundeen now. Then De Spain moved toward him.

Sundeen's eyes shifted momentarily to De Spain. "Pour him a drink."

Frye watched Sundeen and said nothing. He could see that Phil had been drinking. And now he watched him gulp the shot of whisky he was holding.

Sundeen brought the glass down on the bar. "Go ahead . . . drink it."

"Why?"

"We're seeing what kind of a man you are."

"Then what?"

"I think," Sundeen said, slowly, "you're scared to raise the glass."

Frye hesitated. He half turned to the bar, lifted the shot glass with his left hand and drank it in one motion. His eyes flashed back to Sundeen and he saw him grinning now.

"You thought I was going to draw on you," Sundeen said.

"That can work both ways," Frye said.

"If you're man enough." Sundeen grinned. He glanced at De Spain and the bartender filled their glasses again. Sundeen raised his, looking at Frye coolly, then drank it down.

"Why didn't you try?" Sundeen said.

Frye said nothing.

"Maybe you're not fast enough."

Still Frye did not speak.

"Maybe you're just a kid with a big mouth."

"I'm not saying a word."

"A kid with a big mouth and nothing to back it up," Sundeen said evenly.

Frye hesitated.

"Take a drink!"

Frye half turned and drank the shot, using his

left hand, taking his eyes from Sundeen only long enough to swallow the whisky. He watched Sundeen signal again and De Spain refilled their glasses.

"Kirby, you look nervous." Sundeen lounged against the bar with his hip cocked.

"I'm just waiting for you," Frye said.

Sundeen raised his whisky and drank it slowly, then turned to the bar to put the glass down, taking his eyes from Frye for a full five seconds before facing him again.

"There you had plenty of time," Sundeen said. He grinned again. "Plenty of time, but not plenty of guts."

Frye raised his glass unexpectedly and drained it. He saw the look of surprise on Sundeen's face, then saw De Spain fill the glasses again, this time without a signal from Sundeen.

"Now he's drinking for guts," Sundeen said. "A couple more of them and he'll be taking that goddamn warrant out." He drank off his shot quickly. "Kirby, did you bring that warrant with you?"

"Right in my pocket," Frye said. He saw De Spain fill Sundeen's glass again.

"Let's see you serve it."

"Right now?"

"It don't matter when. It's no goddamn good anyway."

"It's got Judge Finnerty's name on it."

Sundeen grinned. "What else you got?"

"A witness outside. Merl White."

"I can handle Merl any seven-day week."

"What if Merl was standing right here?"

"That'd be his second big mistake."

"Everybody's wrong but you," Frye said. He watched Sundeen take another drink. He did not touch his, but said quickly, "We let Tindal and Stedman go, but we're going to lock you up tight until Judge Finnerty's ready for you."

"You're not locking anybody up."

"You'll sit about three weeks waiting for the trial. Then Finnerty'll send you to Yuma for a few years." Frye glanced at De Spain and the bartender slid the bottle along the bar to Sundeen and filled his glass to the top. "Be the driest years you ever spent," Frye said.

Sundeen raised the glass and drank it off, slamming the glass down on the bar. "I'd like to see Finnerty with enough guts to send me to Yuma!"

"You'll see it."

"He's got guts like you have," Sundeen said. "In his mouth."

"Phil," Frye said mildly, "how long have you been bluffing people?"

Sundeen grinned. "You think I'm bluffing?"

"You can shoot quicker, ride faster . . . drink more than anybody else."

"You sound like you don't believe it."

"Well—"

Sundeen reached to the inside edge of the bar and picked up two of the shot glasses that were lined there and placed them next to the one he was using. He pulled the bottle from De Spain's hand and filled them himself. And when the whisky was poured he raised each shot glass in turn, drinking the three of them down without pausing. His eyes squeezed closed and he belched, then he relaxed and rubbed the back of his hand across his mouth.

He looked at Frye. "Now it's your turn."

"I never made any claim as a drinker." He saw Sundeen start to smile and he said to De Spain, "Go ahead," then watched Sundeen again as the bartender filled the glasses. Sundeen lounged against the bar staring back at him.

Frye took his eyes from Sundeen momentarily, picking up the first glass, making himself relax. He glanced at Sundeen, then tossed it down, breathed in as he picked up the second one and drank it, feeling saliva thick in his mouth as he raised the third glass, then gulped it and made himself place the glass on the bar again gently. He breathed slowly with his mouth open, then swallowed to keep the saliva down, feeling the whisky burning in his chest and in his stomach. Nausea that was there momentarily passed off.

Now he felt more sure of himself, but he knew

that it was the whisky and not a feeling he could trust. He could take more, if they did it slowly; but not many more even then. If he had to drink three consecutively again he knew he would not get the last one down. And thinking this he was suddenly less sure of himself. *God, help me. Help me to hold on to myself.* He breathed slowly, making himself relax. *He's had more than you have, but he wants to make a fool out of you and that's all he's thinking about.* He watched Sundeen steadily and it stayed in his mind: *He's drinking more than you are.* De Spain was filling the glasses without waiting for a nod from Sundeen and this also stayed in his mind.

He watched Sundeen take another drink.

Sundeen set the glass down, blowing his breath out slowly, then nodded to Frye. "Your turn."

He lifted the glass, smelling the raw hot smell of the whisky as it reached his mouth and he started to drink.

"Frye!"

The glass came down and he choked on the whisky, coughing, only half seeing Sundeen in his eye-watered vision. He dropped the glass, blinking his eyes, rubbing his left hand over them and now he saw Sundeen. He was laughing, still leaning against the bar. Frye stopped, picking up the glass.

Sundeen said, "You thought that was it, didn't you?"

For a moment Frye watched him in silence. Then he said, "You want the warrant now?"

Sundeen straightened slowly. "Let's see you serve it."

"Without Jordan to help you?"

"I don't need Jordan."

"You did once."

"He was just earning his wages."

"How much did you pay him?"

"Enough."

"Was he worth it?"

"Maybe."

"They say he was pretty good with a gun."

Sundeen grinned. "That's what they say."

Frye's hand dipped into his coat pocket. He brought out Jordan's billfold and threw it down the bar to Sundeen.

"But not good enough," Frye said mildly.

Sundeen glanced at it. "What's that?"

"Jordan's."

"You got him?"

"We buried him."

Sundeen hesitated. "Who?"

"Me."

"What, from behind?"

"Five feet smack in front of him."

"I don't believe it."

"You mean you don't want to believe it."

For the first time, Sundeen had nothing to say. He lifted the whisky glass, drank it and moved his hand slowly putting the glass down.

Frye glanced at De Spain. The bartender filled Sundeen's glass again and Sundeen lifted it and drank it down as soon as the neck of the bottle tilted away from it. Frye held his glass in his hand, but did not drink. "You might as well fill it again," Frye said. "Mr. Sundeen's got some thinking to do."

Sundeen glared at him. "You think you're scaring me?"

"I think you've slowed down some."

"You don't scare nobody."

"Take that whisky, Phil. You'll sound more convincing." He raised his own glass to his lips, seeing Phil tighten, then drank it down, taking his time, and placed the glass on the bar. Sundeen was still tensed.

"Phil, you almost did it that time."

Sundeen gulped his drink. Bringing his glass down he lurched from the bar a half step and had to reach with his right hand to catch the edge of it.

"You almost went for your gun, Phil."

"Listen, you son of a bitch——"

"What stopped you?"

Sundeen hesitated. "I'm waiting to see that warrant."

"You're waiting, but not to see the warrant."

"You do a lot of talking—"

"You're waiting because you don't know what to do."

"Try serving it and I'll show you what I'll do!"

"Jordan had his gun out."

Sundeen flared, "You're a goddamn liar!"

Frye waited momentarily. "Why'd he leave you?"

"That's my business!" Sundeen stared at him with hate in his eyes, then picked up the whisky, spilling some of it, and drank it down. "Your turn!"

Frye kept his eyes on Sundeen as he raised his glass, then took it quickly. Setting it down he saw Sundeen raise another.

Phil drank it, exhaling loudly as he brought the glass down. "Your turn!" he said thickly.

"Phil," Fry said quietly, "I think you're drunk."

"What!"

"You look drunk, that's all."

"I'll drink you into next week!"

Frye shrugged. "You look to me about ready to fall over."

Sundeen's face tightened as he stared at Frye, then seemed to relax though his hand still gripped the edge of the bar. "Now you're calling," Sundeen said, "but you're going to show what you've got, too." Still watching Frye, his hand reached across the bar knocking down some of the shot glasses

lined there, but clutching two and bringing these
back to the middle of the bar. He reached across
and took one more. "I look drunk, huh?" He
glanced at De Spain then. "Fill up!"

De Spain said, "Yes, sir," though his expression
said nothing and he placed the six shot glasses in a
line. He poured whisky into two of them, finishing
what was left in the bottle. Then took a fresh bottle
from the counter behind him and filled the other
four, glancing at Frye as he put the bottle down.

"Well, I've got to see it to believe it," Frye said.

"You'll see it," Sundeen grinned. "Then I'll
watch you do it."

He took the first two standing straight with his
feet spread and planted firmly, then backed up a
step from the bar, holding the edge with his left
hand, as he drank the third one. Frye moved toward him, watching him spill part of the fourth
shot, the whisky running over his chin as he gulped
it. His hand slipped from the bar and he started to
go back, but he lurched forward and caught it
again. His mouth was open gulping in air as he
raised the fifth whisky and as his head jerked back
to take it he spilled most of it. He dropped the glass
to the floor and reached for the sixth one, now
holding his body tight against the bar. He drank it
and brought his hand down, but the glass hit the inside edge of the bar and shattered on the floor. He
held on to the bar now with both hands, swallow-

ing, taking in breaths of air with his mouth open.
He swayed and began to fall back, but he reached
for the bar and fell against it heavily, his arms on
the smooth wet surface, his head down breathing
heavily and now saliva was coming from his
mouth.

Frye stood two steps away from him.

"Phil, you want the warrant now?"

Sundeen lifted his head, squinting at him, blinking his eyes, "Wha—"

"Here's your warrant, Phil."

Sundeen pushed himself from the bar, holding it
with one hand, turning, then stumbling again,
falling against it with his back. He hesitated, studying Frye as if he could not focus his eyes. Suddenly
then, his hand slapped against his holster, fumbling
momentarily, his body swaying away from the bar
as his hand came up with the Colt and waved it toward Frye.

Frye took one step. His left hand covered the
cylinder of the Colt and he twisted, holding Phil's
shirt front with his right hand. The Colt came free
and he pushed Sundeen at the same time.

Sundeen fell heavily against the bar. He held on
momentarily, but it seemed too great an effort and
he let himself slide down to the floor. He rose to his
hands and knees, shaking his head, then sank down
again and did not move.

Frye exhaled slowly and looked at De Spain. "Send him the whisky bill. I'll see that he pays it."

He took the warrant from his pocket and tucked it inside Sundeen's shirt. Then he stooped, pulling Sundeen up over his shoulders and this way he carried him out the front door and across the street. He saw faces, wide open eyes, move from in front of him, but there was not a sound until he reached the steps of the jail. He heard it behind him then, sharp in the stillness, and he knew it was De Spain—

"Didn't even draw his gun!"

Danaher helped him upstairs with Sundeen. They put him in a cell and the last thing Frye remembered was Danaher saying, "Why don't you go in here . . . lie down for a while—"

Danaher went downstairs shaking his head. It was a strange world. He saw Tindal and Stedman turn around as he reached the last step. They must have just come and were talking to Harold Mendez, who was sitting at the desk.

Harold looked up. "They want to talk to Kirby."

"Kirby's taking a rest," Danaher said. "He's had a busy day."

Turn the page for a sneak preview of Elmore Leonard's upcoming western novel,

GUNSIGHTS

The gentleman from *Harper's Weekly*, who didn't know mesquite beans from goat shit, looked up from his reference collection of back issues and said, "I've got it!" Very pleased with himself. "We'll call this affair . . . are you ready? The Early-Moon Feud."

The news reporters in the Gold Dollar shrugged and thought some more, though most of them went on calling it the Rincon Mountains War, which seemed to have enough ring to it.

Somebody said, "What's the matter with the Sweetmary War?" Sweetmary being the name of the mining town where all the gawkers and news reporters had gathered to watch the show. The man from the *St. Louis Globe-Democrat* wanted to call it the Last of The Great Indian Wars. Or—he also mentioned to see how it would sound—the Great Apache Uprising of 1893. Or the Bloody Apache Uprising, etc.

The man from the St. Louis newspaper was reminded that, first, it wasn't an uprising and, sec-

ond, there weren't just Apache Indians up in the mountains; there were also some niggers. The man from St. Louis, being funny, said, "Well, what if we call it the Last of the Great Indian-Nigger Wars?" A man from Florence said, "Well, you have got the chili-pickers in it also. What about them?" Yes, there were some Mexican settlers too, who had been farming up there a hundred years; they were also involved.

What it was, it was a land war.

The LaSalle Mining Company of New Jersey wanted the land. And the Indians from the White Tanks agency, the colored and the Mexicans—all of them actually living up there—wanted it also.

Dana Moon was the Indian Agent at White Tanks, originally established as a reservation for Warm Springs Apaches, or Mimbreños, and a few Lipan and Tonto-Mojave family groups. The agency was located sixteen miles north of Sweetmary and about the same distance west of the San Pedro River. The reservation land was not in dispute. The problem was, many of Moon's Apaches had wandered away from White Tanks—a bleak, young-desert area—to set up rancherías in the mountains. No one, until now, had complained about it.

Brendan Early worked for LaSalle Mining, sort of, with the title Coordinating Manager, Southwest Region, and was living in Sweetmary at the time.

It was said that he and Dana Moon had been up and down the trail together, had shared dry camps and hot corners, and that was why the *Harper's Weekly* man wanted to call it the Early-Moon Feud; which, as you see, had nothing to do with the heavens or astrology.

Nor was there any personal bitterness between them. The question was: What would happen to their bond of friendship, which had tied them together as though on two ends of a short riata, one not venturing too far without running into the other? Would their friendship endure? Or would they now, holding to opposite principles, cut the riata clean and try to kill one another?

Bringing the land question down to personalities, it presented these two as the star attractions: two well-known, soon-to-be-legendary figures about to butt heads. It brought the crowds to Sweetmary to fill up both hotels, the Congress and the Alamosa, a dozen boarding houses, the seven restaurants and thirteen saloons in town. For several weeks this throng swelled the normal population of about four hundred souls, which included the locals, those engaged in commerce, nearby farmers and ranchers and the miners at the Sweetmary Works. Now there were curiosity seekers, gawkers, from all over the Territory and parts of New Mexico.

(Not here yet were the hundred or more gunmen eventually hired by the company to "protect its

leases" and quartered at the mine works. These men were paid, it was said, twenty dollars a week.)

There were newspaper representatives from the *Phoenix Republican, Phoenix Gazette, Yuma Sentinel, Safford Arizonian, Tucson Star, Florence Enterprise, Prescott Courier, Cococino Sun, Clifton Copper Era, Graham County Bulletin, Tombstone Prospector, St. Louis Globe-Democrat, Chicago Times* and the *New York Tribune*.

Harper's Weekly had hired the renowned photographer C. S. Fly of Tombstone to cover the war with his camera, the way he had pictorially recorded Crook's campaign against Geronimo and his renegade Apaches.

C. S. Fly set up a studio on LaSalle Street and there presented "showings" of many of his celebrated photographs of Indians, hangings, memorial parades and well-known personages, including Geronimo, former president Garfield and several of Brendan Early and Dana Moon. The two photos that were perhaps best known showed them at Fort Huachuca, June 16, 1887, with a prisoner they had brought in that day.

There they were, six years ago:

Brendan Early, in his hip-cocked cavalry pose. First Lieutenant of the 10th at Huachuca but wearing civilian dress, a very tight-fitting light-colored suit of clothes; bare-headed to show his brown wavy hair; a silky-looking kerchief at his throat; a

matched pair of Smith and Wesson .44 Russians, butt-forward in Army holsters, each with the flap cut off; cavalry boots wiped clean for the pose; Brendan holding his Spencer carbine like a walking cane, palm resting on the upraised barrel. He seems to be trying to look down his nose like an Eastern dandy while suppressing a grin that shows clearly in his eyes.

In contrast:

Dana Moon with his dark, drooping mustache that makes him appear sad; hat brim straight and low over his eyes, a bulge in his bony countenance indicating the ever-present plug of tobacco; dark suit of clothes and a polka-dot neckerchief. Dana's .44 Colt's revolver is in a shoulder rig, a glint of it showing. He grips a Big-fifty Sharps in one hand, a sawed-off 12-gauge Greener in the other. All those guns for a man who looks so mild, so solemn.

Between the two:

Half a head shorter is a one-eyed Mimbreño Apache named Loco. What a funny-looking little man, huh? Black eyepatch, black stringy hair hanging from the bandana covering his head, he looks like a pirate of some kind, wearing an old dirty suit-coat and a loincloth. But don't laugh at him. Loco has killed many people and went to Washington to meet Grover Cleveland when times were better.

The caption beneath the photo, which appeared that year in *Harper's Weekly*, reads:

Lt. Brendan Early   Loco   Dana Moon
Two Famous Heroes of the West with a Captive
Red Devil

There was also a photo of the Two Famous Heroes standing on either side of an attractive fairhaired young lady in a torn and dirty cotton dress; she is wearing a man's shirt over her quite filthy attire, the shirt unbuttoned, hanging free. The young lady does not seem happy to be posing for her picture that day at Fort Huachuca. She looks as though she might walk up to the camera and kick it over.

The caption beneath this one reads:

Lt. Brendan Early   Katherine McKean   Dana Moon
Following Her Ordeal, Katy McKean
Gratefully Thanks Her Rescuers

In the *Harper's Weekly* article there was mention of a 10th Cavalry sergeant by the name of Bo Catlett, a Negro. Though he did not appear in either of the photographs, Sergeant Catlett had accompanied the Two Famous Heroes in their quest to apprehend the Apache warchief, Loco, and shared credit for bringing him in and rescuing the McKean girl. In the article, Sergeant Catlett was asked where he had gotten the name Bo. "I believe it short for 'Boy,' suh," was his reply.

Not many days before the photographs were